NOT A SINGLE CLUE IN DARING RUBY HEIST

INTERNATIONAL CRIME-FIGHTING AGENCIES LEFT SCRATCHING THEIR HEADS

"IT'S LIKE A MAGICIAN MADE IT DISAPPEAR," ANNOUNCED THE CHIEF INVESTIGATOR. "I'VE NEVER SEEN SUCH A CLEAN HEIST."

DARING BURGLAR LIKELY HAS DOZENS OF SECRET IDENTITIES

BAFFLED DETECTIVES SAY EVIDENCE POINTS TO SINGLE BURGLAR WITH MANY DISGUISES

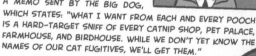

"AND THEY'RE NOT YOUR EVERYDAY OFF-THE-RACK DISGUISES," SAYS ONE INVESTIGATOR. "THIS THIEF HAS A FABULOUS FASHION SENSE."

CENTRAL CANINE INTELLIGENCE AGENCY RAMPS UP

CCIA ANNOUNCES PLAN TO BEEF UP **PAW AND ORDER** FOLLOWING GLOBAL CAT CRIME SPREE

THE MEW YORK TIMES UNCOVERED A MEMO SENT BY THE BIG DOG, WHICH STATES: "WHAT I WANT FROM EACH AND EVERY POOCH IS A HARD-TARGET SNIFF OF EVERY CATNIP SHOP, PET PALACE, FARMHOUSE, AND BIRDHOUSE. WHILE WE DON'T YET KNOW THE NAMES OF OUR CAT FUGITIVES, WE'LL GET THEM."

Praise for SNAZZY CAT CAPERS

"I want to be Ophelia when I grow up! And I want Oscar to be my BFF—Best Fishy Friend! *Snazzy Cat Capers* is fabulous, funny, and fin-tastic fun with illustrations that pounce off the page."

—MO O'HARA, *NEW YORK TIMES*–BESTSELLING AUTHOR OF THE MY BIG FAT ZOMBIE GOLDFISH SERIES

"Classy bad girl Ophelia is as funny as she is furry . . . She's the pussycat love child of James Bond and Zsa Zsa Gabor, and who can't love that?"

—*KIRKUS REVIEWS*

"More than a just sharply dressed classy kitty . . . Ophelia and Fishgerald squabble and lob quips with amusing ease."

—*BULLETIN OF THE CENTER FOR CHILDREN'S BOOKS*

SNAZZY
CAT CAPERS

DEANNA KENT

ILLUSTRATED BY NEIL HOOSON

[Imprint]
MAKE YOUR MARK
NEW YORK

SQUARE FISH

An imprint of Macmillan Publishing Group, LLC
120 Broadway, New York, NY 10271
mackids.com

Our books may be purchased in bulk for promotional, educational, or business use.
Please contact your local bookseller or the Macmillan Corporate and Premium
Sales Department at (800) 221-7945 ext. 5442 or by email at
MacmillanSpecialMarkets@macmillan.com.

Library of Congress Control Number: 2018936703

ISBN 978-1-250-21114-9 (paperback)   ISBN 978-1-250-14342-6 (ebook)

[Imprint]
MAKE YOUR MARK

@ImprintReads
Originally published in the United States by Imprint
First Square Fish edition, 2020
Book designed by Eileen Savage
Illustrations by Neil Hooson
Imprint logo designed by Amanda Spielman
Square Fish logo designed by Filomena Tuosto

1 3 5 7 9 10 8 6 4 2

LEXILE: 680L

FFBI Official Bulletin
Attention, cat burglars: Book thievery is not deemed honorable by the Furry Feline Burglary
Institute. Those who do not comply will be cursed with catnip shortages and dog breath.

For Sam, Max, Zach, Jake, Jackson, Ethan, Ella, Colton, and Anna—
and for anyone who has ever secretly (or not so secretly) wanted
to be a snazzy cat burglar with lots of guts and awesome gadgets.

SNAZZY CAT CAPERS

FUR-WORD

JUST WHO IS OPHELIA VON HAIRBALL Ⅴ OF BURGLARIA?

Crime Magazine, the National Scratching Post, and Vanity Fur call her "the mysterious solo cat burglar who's taking the world by storm with style and sass." An elite member of the Furry Feline Burglary Institute, Ophelia is a thief extraordinaire who follows a timeless, honorable code to keep cat burglary classy. Everyone asks me what she's really like behind the mask. Think of a fluffy James Bond with a love for diamonds, disguises, and double dares.

—Oscar F. Gold (Inventor #17)

"You can't possibly be your best if you haven't had a manicure. Or if you're a dog."

—Ophelia von Hairball V

1

REBEL WITH SOME (LOVELY) CLAWS

The gold-leaf invitations had been delivered by white doves. Crystal chariots drove A-list guests to the front doors. Ball gowns glimmered with gems. It had been a long time since Ophelia von Hairball V attended a masquerade ball at a castle, but in her disguise, she sparkled as brightly as everyone else—probably more.

"Hold on." A security guard stopped her. "Your

invitation seems *different*." He shone his flashlight to take a closer look.

"Different? Really?" she inquired. She quickly shifted her attention to the guard's outfit. "Your uniform is superb." Ophelia loved a good costume as much as a good forgery, and her forged invitation was purr-fectly identical to the real ones—with one important difference: She'd crafted it with a higher-quality gold. "But your wig seems crooked. May I fix it for you?" she asked.

The guard frowned. "Crooked? I don't like crooked."

"Sometimes crooked is okay"—Ophelia grinned—"but never for paintings or hair." He let her straighten his wig.

"Your invitation looks fine. Sorry to keep you waiting. We had an attempted robbery a few days ago and we're on high alert." The guard waved her in.

PURRRR. Inside the doorway, Ophelia's ringtone was drowned out by an orchestra playing "O Fur-tuna" and the complaints of spoiled guests upset that their jewels were too heavy.

Ophelia opened her handbag to sneak a peek at her phone. The Furry Feline Burglary Institute! Normally, Ophelia von Hairball V *pounced* on a call from the FFBI. But just yesterday, she'd sent her sixteenth inventor packing. Sixteenth! It was a record for the most inventors *ever* returned to the FFBI,

so she was sure the Feline Director (code name: MEW) was calling to scold her.

PURRRR. Not a big fan of scoldings, Ophelia silenced her phone. Maybe she'd call Director MEW back tomorrow to tell her side of the story. She'd sent Norman—the sixteenth inventor—packing for a lot of *very* good reasons. For example, he was obsessed with knock-knock jokes, his off-key singing tended to attract stray animals, and if he saw a bug, he froze like a statue. But most importantly, Ophelia fired him because she liked to work alone. The FFBI should know by now that she didn't want or need a helper. She was the greatest cat burglar in the world—a solo act.

Ophelia took a deep breath, tightened her mask, and elegantly glided into the crowded room. In no time at all, she was twirling around the dance floor, moving toward the staircase. But she wasn't there to mingle. Instead, her grand plan was to sneak upstairs and liberate a sparkling emerald tiara from its cold, steel safe.

Truth be told, the last thing Ophelia *needed* was another tiara. Recently, she'd been bored with her tiara pile, so she'd returned (anonymously, of course) several dozen to their former owners.

But *this* tiara was special. Every month, the FFBI sent out special challenges to the elite cat burglars. Practice makes purr-fect, after all. The cat who checked the most items off the list was the winner. Pierre, her cousin and archrival, had double-dared Ophelia to try to get the emerald tiara because he didn't think she could pull it off with the panache she was infamous for. Ophelia desperately wanted to show him that she could. And once the tiara was in her paws, she planned to flaunt her burglar-tastic superiority during the next FFBI meeting.

A waiter in a black tuxedo and matching gloves stopped to offer Ophelia goodies from a silver tray. "Caviar?"

"Oh." She licked her lips. "You've discovered my weakness." She was tempted to stop and have a little snack. "What I wouldn't give for a taste," she admitted, "but I'm on a rather tight deadline this evening. I have to leave the party early. Alas, no time for treats."

Ophelia noted the waiter's silk gloves and flashed her most charming grin. "Those gloves are so lovely. . . . May I?"

"Keep them! They give me the worst rash!" he exclaimed.

Ophelia handed him a generous tip. She put on the gloves, then poked her claws through the tops of the fingers.

"Divine!" she whispered. A purr-fect fit. Plus, she wouldn't leave any paw prints! Ophelia waltzed through the crowd and checked the time. It was eleven thirty. She only had until midnight to get the tiara and exit the castle.

She discreetly checked the castle's blueprint, which she had printed on her fan. Then, with a practiced eye (and the longest eyelashes in the land), Ophelia scoped out the ballroom. She noted the objects that might help or hinder her escape.

Dozens of twinkle-light ropes dangled from the upper-floor railings. On the dance floor, hundreds of guests formed a twirling rainbow of silk and lace. In the corner, a two-story chocolate fountain was a sweet magnet to a crowd of jet-setters. All over, sleepy security guards half-heartedly scanned the room.

Ophelia climbed the stairs to the second floor. Just down the hallway was a tiny room disguised as a closet. Inside was a safe.

It was really no wonder that her cousin Pierre hadn't figured out a way to crack it—the safe was an old-fashioned design. The *second* best burglar at the FFBI, Pierre turned up his nose at anything classic (or classy, for that matter). Ophelia thought he was a disgrace to the cat burglar profession.

The FFBI had been around for centuries, and their cat burglars (especially the elite) treated each heist as an opportunity to hone their skills. But it wasn't easy; there were rules to follow. A great cat burglar needed to be stealthy and smart, and perform purr-fect crimes! It was also an unwritten rule that the classiest cat burglars didn't *keep* the priceless objects they pilfered. (Although it sometimes took a little while to return very, very pretty things to their owners.) For a good cat burglar, it was all about the chase.

Even though Pierre was an elite cat burglar, he didn't bother with the honor code among kitty thieves. Pierre had always preferred brute force over brains. He did things the easy way, not the right way. Ophelia thought his careless habits were dangerous for the whole FFBI organization. She never missed a chance to show him that a superior cat burglar could win both small challenges and big competitions with charm.

It took Ophelia only thirty seconds, a doctor's stethoscope, and a gentle paw to crack the safe. When she heard the combination click into place, she ever-so-carefully swung the door open.

"Well, well." She gazed at the tiara. It was beautifully lit by moonbeams. "Aren't you just a *glorious* trinket?" Plucking the sparkling piece from its pressure-sensitive velvet pad, she placed it atop her head. It was a lovely fit and purr-fectly matched her gown—which, of course, had been her plan.

She did a fast calculation and guessed that it would take the castle's tired security guards at least sixty seconds to respond to the safe's silent alarm. That was plenty of time to make her escape. Using the twinkle-lights as a rope was the best way to gracefully (and quickly) get back down to the main floor.

Ophelia landed on the main level and got just a few feet across the dance floor when a guest in head-to-toe purple sequins blocked her path. "Darling! Where in heavens did you come from? And WHO made your mask? Calvin Claw? Kitty Klum? It's outstanding!"

"Neither. I craft most of my own disguises . . . er, outfits. I try *very hard* not to buy things."

A small army of now-alert security guards came into view. They were standing by the door, looking rather frantic. Ophelia sensed that they were moments away from locking down the castle.

"Please excuse me." Ophelia curtsied. "I need some air." *And a distraction.*

Twirling back through the dancers, Ophelia made herself invisible among the crowd and headed to the chocolate fountain. There, she set the fountain's speed to *high* and used her new gloves to lock it in place. A few seconds later, chocolate flowed at an incredible pace . . . and then overflowed. Few things were more distracting than waterfalls of liquid chocolate! As guests started slipping on the chocolate-covered floor, rich laughter turned into gooey groans.

The chaos gave Ophelia the few extra seconds she needed to slip unseen out of the castle. As always, she was exactly on time for her preplanned helicopter pickup. Being on time is, after all, a sign of class—and one of her trademark moves.

During the journey home, Ophelia catnapped. She dreamed of a fairy-tale genie in a shiny gold bottle who told her to make a wish. Her dreams usually came true—so she cleverly wished for another wish.

What she got instead was an unexpected surprise.

"They say good things come to those
who wait. But who likes waiting?"

—Ophelia von Hairball V

2

CAREFUL WHAT YOU WISH FUR

Back at her lair, Ophelia was forced to let Director MEW of the FFBI rant a bit. "Number four was returned for 'not French-braiding the hair that sprouted from his ears.' Number nine was rejected for 'not fully appreciating my genius.' Number twelve was sent back for 'throwing fart-bombs in her sleep.' How does one even 'throw' farts, Ophelia?! And what was wrong with

Norman? He had no ear hair! He didn't withhold compliments! And no gas issues. In fact, I hand-picked him! He was purrrr-fect for you!"

As MEW ranted, her face pinched and squashed in ways Ophelia had never seen it pinch and squash before. Ophelia knew MEW wasn't finished, and she knew better than to interrupt. "Ophelia—sixteen inventors! In one year! It's disgraceful."

Over the video conference call, Ophelia tried *very hard* to look *very sorry.* "I'm sorry, MEW, but I work best alone."

MEW tried to stay calm. "You don't get it, do you? You can't just keep returning purr-fectly brilliant inventors! There was nothing wrong with Norman!"

"I disagree! Besides his bug phobia, I put up with a *lot* of knock-knock jokes! But the big-gest issue here," Ophelia pleaded, "is that we all know I don't need a sidekick inventor *and I don't want one.*"

"Since last year, official FFBI policy mandates that every agent has an inventor. There are no exceptions. What's the FFBI's motto, Ophelia?"

"Purr-fect crimes."

"Precisely! But that's not easy! Our purr-fect crime rate is going down—cats are getting caught. The Central Canine Intelligence Agency is definitely ramping up. As you know, they have a weird habit of marking their territory—they put their CCIA logo on everything, so we've been able to detect their increased presence all over the world! Every cat operative has to be more careful. And that means each of us needs a paw-rtner in crime."

Ophelia knew MEW was right about the increasing threat of the CCIA. Those dogs would stop at nothing to bring down the FFBI. They just didn't understand the genius and skill behind the work of the feline thieves. But even if they were smart, Ophelia had never met any dog who was a match

for her brains. She absolutely did *not* need an inventor to slow her down.

"Can we please talk about this later, Director
MEW? I'm exhausted
from last night's
long journey.
Would you like to
see the lovely tiara
I picked up in the
Alps? I won the latest
challenge!"

Oddly, MEW didn't look like she cared *at all*
about Ophelia's new tiara. "Lovely or not, I don't
know why you're wasting time in the Alps with
that small challenge when you should be in *Paris*.
Surely a measly tiara is not worth losing the big
competition!"

Ophelia thought she must have misheard.
"Uh, *pardonnez-moi?* Paris?"

"Every other agent—including Pierre—is a
whole forty-eight hours ahead of you. Time is
running out!"

Ophelia felt the blood rush from the tips of her claws into her gorgeous ears. Pierre? Her archrival was *getting ahead*? She had no clue what MEW was talking about, but the thought of Pierre beating her at *anything* made her furious. "Competition?! Director, what do you mean? Why am I supposed to be in Paris?"

"It's the—"

"*HISS!* I apologize." Ophelia had to cut MEW off. "Please excuse me for one moment. There's a *very* persistent and pesky stranger at my door."

MEW smiled. "Oh, please answer it. I should go. Call me if you have any questions. And remember, Ophelia—the inventor is mandatory. No refunds! No returns! No exchanges! Au revoir!"

"You could say I'm a mix of Einstein and Catwoman. But I'm snazzier than both of them."

—Ophelia von Hairball V

3

P.U.G. & PRICKLES

At the door was a lone goldfish in a tank of water with high-tech gadgets. He seemed to know Ophelia quite well since he didn't even introduce himself. He bowed and declared, "Your wish is granted! I've arrived!"

Suddenly, Ophelia remembered her dream and clutched her head in her paws. She had wished for a wish. . . . Instead, here was a *fish*.

"Did you say, 'you're mine'?"

"Yes. Mine." The fish looked flustered. "Well, I'm yours. And you're mime. Oops, I mean *mine*. You're not a mime. Are you a mime? Well, anyhow, we belong to each other. Partners!"

"Sorry—I didn't quite catch your name?" Ophelia inquired, hoping he was simply a very enthusiastic salesfish selling door-to-door.

"Oscar Fishgerald Gold of the FFBI. Senior inventor at your service!" He beamed at her. "I've been sent by—"

Too flustered to remember her manners, Ophelia interrupted him. "Oscar, do you sing?"

"Er, badly. But not in public."

"Do you tell knock-knock jokes?"

Ophelia wished she could close her eyes and make this all go away. "Do you burp the alphabet, chew your nails and spit them out on the kitchen table, or breathe loudly during nap time?"

Oscar didn't miss a beat. "I wish, never, and does the occasional gurgle count as breathing loudly?" He smiled, and Ophelia wondered if he was toying with her. "May I please come in now?"

Ophelia considered saying no, but she thought she saw Thug—the new, nosy dog next door—poke his head under the fence. The last thing she needed was for that mutt to chomp the new fish inventor. MEW would blame her if anything happened to him. Ophelia yanked Oscar and his suitcase inside and closed the door.

Oscar studied her less-than-thrilled face. "Listen, Ophelia: I know I'm the seventeenth inventor assigned to you, and that means you're picky about your partners. I respect that. If you give me a chance, you'll see that I can help you become an even better cat burglar than you already are." He smiled. "Go ahead and give me a challenge!"

Ophelia closed her eyes in a long blink. She

wanted to challenge him to disappear, but MEW would be oh-so angry. . . .

"Okay, okay. You want something to do? Go fetch the mail."

Oscar hesitated. "No offense, but I'm a *senior* inventor. I have more IQ points than you have shoes. I'm not a dog and I don't *fetch* things!"

An interesting thought gripped Ophelia. Perhaps if she gave the overeager fish *nothing* to do, maybe he'd get bored and go away on his own.

"Fine." She shrugged and flicked her whiskers. "Don't worry about it. I'll get my own mail. Why don't you just relax? There's really not much to do around here."

I'VE GOT AN IDEA... I'M GOING TO **BUILD** YOU SOMETHING THAT WILL FETCH YOUR MAIL...

AND SO MUCH MORE!

OKAY. IF YOU SAY SO.

INVENTOR AT WORK.

DO NOT ENTER.

BANG   BAM

CRASH

SAW

INVENTOR AT WORK.
DO NOT ENTER.

WHIR

INVENTOR AT WORK.
DO NOT ENTER.

WAIT FOR IT...

TA-DA! MAY I PRESENT YOUR VERY OWN **PERSONAL ULTRA GADGET.**

LET'S CALL IT **P.U.G.** FOR SHORT.

Ophelia dropped her phone. "What the—? Do you always say 'ta-da'? And is that wretched dog-robot design a joke?"

"Yes, I suppose I do say 'ta-da' quite a lot. Like a magician. However, P.U.G. is no joke." Oscar grinned. "It's quite a good likeness to that dog next door, wouldn't you say?"

"Listen, fish: I could drain your tank at any moment."

"Let's allow P.U.G. to prove its worthiness."
Oscar whistled. "P.U.G.! Go get the mail!" The
robot bounded outside at top speed.

When the mechanical abomination didn't
return for several minutes, Ophelia poked her
nose outside to see what was happening. Its head
was in the dirt, its metal butt sticking straight
up, and all four supersonic paws were frantically
clawing up Ophelia's award-winning rosebush.

"Your dumb dog-bot invention is broken!" she
yelled to Oscar. "You asked for the mail and it's
digging up my garden!"

"Impossible," Oscar answered. "I coded it
myself. P.U.G. is perfectly programmed to be
quite doglike and very obedient."

Suddenly, P.U.G.'s tail started wagging and it
emerged from the freshly dug hole with a small
bag in its mouth. Proud and panting, it dragged
the sack through the dirt and dropped it in front
of Ophelia. Curious, she opened it and reached
inside to retrieve the contents.

"*YEOW! MEOW!*" Her delicate paws became

victims of several
rose thorn prickles.
But her pain was
quickly replaced with
puzzlement. The bag
was full of dozens of
unopened letters—all
addressed to her!

Who would steal her
mail and bury it in her
garden? And why?!

"There are only three things you really need in life: a big dream, a terrific plan, and a fabulous shoe collection."

—Ophelia von Hairball V

4

A PURR-FECT STORM

What's in the bag?" Oscar was jumping out of his fins with curiosity. "Giant opals? Priceless coins? Secret love letters?"

"No, you nosy fish. They are . . . invitations." Ophelia could hardly believe it. With each letter she opened, new waves of anger curled her whiskers. After a few moments, all of her fur stood on end. She pulled out one envelope after the other.

Every one had the FFBI seal on the corner. "This bag is filled with invitations and reminders about the latest and greatest Furry Feline Burglary Institute Purr-fect Heist Competition! The one that's happening in Paris RIGHT NOW! The one that I can't win, because I didn't even know about it!"

FFBI

DEAR ELITE CAT BURGLAR,

YOU HAVE BEEN INVITED TO PARTICIPATE IN THE

FFBI'S FIFTH ANNUAL PURR-FECT HEIST COMPETITION

THIS YEAR: STEAL THE RARE HIMALAYAN DIAMOND*
FROM THE FAMED, HEAVILY GUARDED
BELLE MEW-SEUM IN PARIS, FRANCE.

THE FIRST FFBI AGENT TO
HAND IN THE DIAMOND WINS THE

PURR-FECT HEIST TROPHY

AND WILL BE RECOGNIZED AS THE
FFBI'S BEST CAT BURGLAR.

DEADLINE IS **12:01 A.M.** (EST),
OCTOBER 17 AT THE FFBI OFFICE IN
BRUSSELS, BELGIUM (LOCAL TIME 6:01 A.M.).

*WINNER SUBJECT TO GEM AUTHENTICATION
INSPECTION BY A CERTIFIED FFBI GEMOLOGIST.

"Do you want to sit down?" Oscar pulled a fuzzy cushion over for her. "You look like your blood might just boil."

"There's no time to sit, Oscar. There's hardly time to breathe. The contest ends in under TWO DAYS!" She examined the postmarks. "My mail has been buried in the garden for weeks!"

"Intriguing," Oscar puzzled. "Why would someone try to prevent you from participating in the competition? Also, why doesn't the FFBI use e-mail?"

"They do. But I don't enjoy e-mail. It's easier to tamper with and not as classy as old-fashioned mail." Ophelia rolled her eyes. "Besides, the catnip spam I get is beyond ridiculous. Don't get me wrong. I like high-tech things. But when there's a choice, I always request the classic option."

Oscar peered into the bag. "Anything else in there?" There was one last, lone letter at the bottom.

"Hey!" Oscar exclaimed. "I've seen his picture

at FFBI HQ. He's a bully. None of the inventors like to work with him."

"GROWL. Pierre von Rascal of Thievesylvania, my cousin, is the least charming criminal around."

"Oh!" Oscar clapped his fins together. "A family rivalry! Such drama! I think his eyebrows are impressive. . . ."

"This is no ordinary rivalry, fish-face. Pierre's jealousy of me started when we were barely more than small balls of fur. He once stole my favorite Captain Claw-some action figure. He still has it!"

"But that must have been so long ago," Oscar replied.

"Oh, it just gets worse and worse! He's always mad at me because I win. Do you want to know why I win? Because he's sloppy, and I do things right!" Just then, P.U.G. licked Ophelia's face. "UGH! Please program that robot to *never* lick me. I suppose I don't really have time to tell you a bunch of old Ophelia versus Pierre rivalry stories. I've got to figure out how to get ahead when I'm already so far behind."

Ophelia's eyes narrowed and she paced the room. The thought of Pierre stealing these letters for weeks and weeks made her want to cough up a big, fat hairball.

"My cousin is out to sabotage me and break my winning streak. I've always won the FFBI's Purr-fect Heist Competition!" She took a deep breath to counteract the hissy fit she felt coming on. "Can you check to see if anyone's successfully stolen the Paris diamond yet? If not, I need to get there ASAP."

Ophelia knew that if she could get to Paris quickly, then with the right tools and the help of a few international allies, she could win the contest, get her prize, and keep her number-one spot.

Oscar checked the global databases. "The diamond still appears to be at the Mew-seum. We have a chance!"

Ophelia studied the Mew-seum's blueprints. A few ideas about a very grand heist started to brew in her mind.

"I can do this," Ophelia muttered out loud. "I'm going to need a grab-and-switch gadget— one that's the exact weight of the Himalayan diamond. There are invisible lasers surrounding the pedestal; I'll need some way to see them. If I can get into the room and avoid the alarms, I should be able to grab that gorgeous gem and waltz out the front door with style. I do love a good heist where I can walk out the front door. . . ."

Oscar jumped into action. "That's the winning attitude! I'll start making gadgets while you book our passage to Paris."

"'Our' passage?" Ophelia's purr-fectly manicured eyebrows shot up to the ceiling. "I need gadgets for sure. But *we* do not need a travel plan. Only *I* do."

Even though Ophelia was almost two full days behind Pierre and all the other agents, she knew she was the superior contender. Her stomach fluttered. This particular competition was such a wonderful thrill! Nothing worth having was ever easy to obtain. But she was prepared to win at any

cost, because there was absolutely no way that she would allow her cousin to knock her from the number-one spot at the FFBI.

It was time to get to Paris and steal the giant diamond.

**"Know your friends. Know your anemones.
And always know where the best snacks are."**

—Ophelia von Hairball V

5

PAWS-ITIVELY PREPARED

REMAINING

Successful heists are only as good as the brains behind them. Under normal circumstances, Ophelia prepared for months prior to every criminal escapade. Plans were crafted! Disguises were created! Blueprints were studied, and global allies were sent big boxes of treats in anticipation of their generous help.

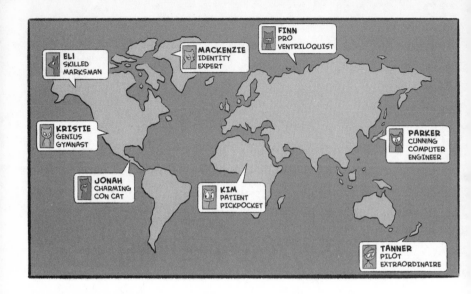

But because of Pierre's trickery, Ophelia had hardly any time for secret travel or elaborate plans. She had to get to Paris fast. She got to work booking first-class airline tickets. "The last name is von Hairball. That's V-O-N H-A-I-R-B-A-L-L."

"Pssst! Hello! Excuse me, please." Oscar interrupted her phone call with a very loud, dramatic whisper. "I know an international heist-master like you must have a ton of fake identities." His brow furrowed with concern. "I don't think you should be using your real name! We should assume that your evil cousin is watching your every move!"

Ophelia shushed him, but he was persistent.

"Oh dear. He'll try to set you up! What if you go to jail? You would not be happy in prison, Ophelia. They use *very* uncomfortable fabric for their uniforms! Plus, orange isn't at all complementary to your fur tone. . . ."

"Oscar, stop. I'm simply booking *decoy* travel to trick Pierre if he's watching me."

"Ooooh. OOOOH! You're entirely too clever...." He smiled. "So... what's the real plan?"

"Shhhh. Curiosity didn't kill the cat . . . but it could come after the fish! Please leave me be. Don't you have things to invent?"

Oscar crumpled. "Ophelia! I'm your biggest fan, and I'm *craving* action and adventure! When the FFBI assigned me to you, they said I'd be out in the field more. Also," he confided, straightening his tie, "Paris is perfect, because I love fashion. And I need to learn some French! *Wee-wee, mon-see-yur. Le pwa-sawn dore say troo-vay oh ban-an-ee-air.*"

"'*The gold fish is in the banana stand*'? Do you even know what you're saying? FISH! STOP! You're hurting my ears!"

Ophelia sighed. Overall, she thought Oscar seemed like a nice fish. He'd certainly done his homework and knew a lot about her. She wanted to be honest with him. "Fin-boy, even if I wanted you to come—which I don't—the last thing I need is to be taking care of you and your little tank lab. All the splooshing and splashing would be counterproductive to my solo stealth operation."

Oscar stood tall. "Counterproductive? Oh no! I'd never be a burden to you. My S.P.I.T. is totally portable, not to mention sploosh-proof."

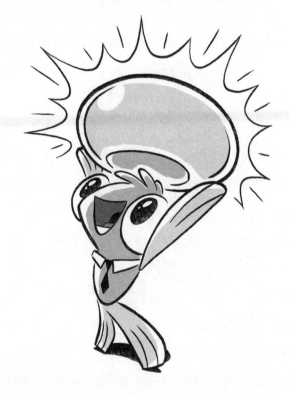

"Spit?" Ophelia asked. "How crass."

"S.P.I.T. is short for Small Portable Inter-water Tank. It will sustain me on dry land for weeks at a time. It has a sleek design, too."

Ophelia was speechless. Oscar mistook her silence for jealousy. "Oh, don't be sad! I've also made you something! . . . Ta-da! A scuba suit. It's quite fashionable and coated with a highly water-repellent compound I came up with."

The cat shook her head back and forth. "NO, NO, NO, fish-flake. Scuba suits aren't my thing—fashionable or not. I'm not a fan of water. Anyhow, if you've studied my criminal career, you'll know that I'm a solo act. I don't need a companion, buddy, or sidekick. I'll steal the diamond alone. Now, do you have the gadgets I asked for?"

He sighed and handed over a small silver box. "Of course I do. When you get into the room with the jewel, hit the purple button. It will release a specially formulated purple dust concoction. The dust will hide you from the cameras and also let you see any invisible laser beams."

"Why purple?" Ophelia asked.

"Just for fun. You might want to design an outfit around it," Oscar told her.

"Impressive," Ophelia admitted. "I always say the devil is in the details. It's the same weight as the diamond?"

"Yes. Once the dust is released, the box will be exactly 3,501.17 carats—or approximately 24.700027472 ounces—the weight of the Himalayan diamond. It's so easy. Push the button, perform a very

RELEASES PLUME OF PURPLE SMOKE (GOOD FOR EXPOSING LASER BEAMS)

precise grab-and-switch move, and then take the diamond. The box is untraceable."

Oscar looked at her with respect. "Do a lot of cat burglars still do the grab-and-switch? It seems so marvelously old-fashioned."

Ophelia was flattered. "Not many, in fact." She was proud of her skills. "I may be the only cat burglar left in the world who can pull it off. But I do love well-timed moves. Did you know I trained with the world-renowned Mewdini? A grab-and-switch is difficult to perfect but worth learning."

"I did know that," Oscar admitted. "I really have researched and memorized your heists. Every single one. Your moves—and your disguises—are famous around the globe."

Secretly, she was pleased that he knew her pedigree. "What's the tiny gold button for?"

He looked embarrassed. "Oh. Uh, it's nothing.

Sort of my personal signature. I put bonus features in all the gadgets I make. Just for fun. A 'deluxe Oscar surprise,' if you will. There's even one on P.U.G. But you should leave the gold button alone. Don't *ever* push it unless I tell you to!"

Ophelia scowled, fighting her natural curious instincts. She handed it back to Oscar. "Oh, I won't. I'm not a fan of surprises. But I want to know what it does. So *you'll* push it—now."

Oscar knew he wasn't going to change her mind, so he took the box and closed his eyes, then reluctantly tapped the gold button. A whirling tornado formed above his head and spun him around and around. After a few seconds, the spontaneous wind stopped and he collapsed in a dizzy heap. "I like to do different little things every time. That handcrafted, artisan tornado was my first attempt at a portable mini weather storm."

Ophelia looked at him and sighed. "I won't *ever* press the gold button," she vowed, knowing that probably wasn't true. (She was as curious as any cat.) "And one more thing, Oscar . . . would you happen to have a pattern for an aerodynamic wingsuit somewhere?" she asked. "You can use the gorgeous silk I bought in Japan."

"Yes, of course." With a wobble, he stood up. "I'll *make* you a pattern—one of a kind, of course— and P.U.G. can quickly sew it for you. But first, please tell me your plan. How are you going to sneak your new gadget past the rigid Mew-seum security? Do you have insiders? Contacts? Spies?"

"Normally, I'd have help. But thanks to Pierre, there won't be time." She went to her storage room and lugged out a very large crate. Oscar tagged along right behind her. "You're crowding me," she told him. "I'm trying to get ready."

His eyes widened. "But I want to know your plan!"

Ophelia sensed that he would keep asking until she told him. "See this luxurious, spa-like crate big enough for one cat and her accessories? THIS is how I'm traveling to Paris! By express airmail."

"I don't understand. No stealth helicopter? No supersonic jet?"

"No. Pierre will be expecting that. Just look at the address! This crate will be shipped—expressly, of course—directly *into* the Mew-seum in Paris where the jewel is kept. Get it? When I open the lid, I'll already be inside the Mew-seum and past entrance security. I'll have everything I need to nab the famed Himalayan diamond. Then I'll go to Brussels to collect my FFBI trophy. It's genius, if I do say so myself!"

Oscar paused and studied her face. "Do you ever feel sorry for Pierre? Would it be so bad for him to win one time?"

Ophelia took a breath, smoothed her tail, and put on her travel robe. "Yes, it would be so bad. I need to win this competition. I'm well on my way to breaking the world record for the highest number of successful heists sanctioned by the FFBI. My legacy will live on in the Hall of Fame. I'll be forever known as the best and classiest cat burglar."

Ophelia hopped into the crate, which coincidentally contained a spa-style chair, luxury rug, and small trunk for all her burglary necessities. "Good-bye, Oscar. Have a relaxing week. If you're bored, please go visit MEW. Just make sure to lock up before you leave my lair."

For a moment, Oscar had a glimmer of admiration for her in his bulgy eyes, but it quickly died and Ophelia saw something else. Concern? Fear?

"I hate to rub your fur the wrong way, but before you put the top on that crate, I need to tell

you that your plan might be flawed." He continued, "I mean, in theory, it's brilliant—like you!"
He gulped nervously. "However, scientifically
speaking, you're going to take your last breaths
in that little travel spa crate of yours." He popped
his small body up and down to look Ophelia right
in the eyes.

> "Always know what you do well.
> Then do more of it."
>
> —Ophelia von Hairball V

6

FIN-VENTOR ON THE MOVE

Last breaths? Never make it alive? Ophelia checked her watch (an antique trinket she'd nabbed during a Scottish castle heist). She only had *ten minutes* until her travel crate was to be picked up. Her gut was telling her that the fish was being overly dramatic. However, she didn't want to die—or for Pierre to get the diamond.

"All right, all right!" she gave in with a huff. "Just hurry up and tell me what's wrong with this crate!"

Oscar looked smug. "According to my calculations, the airhole circumferences aren't large enough to give you a steady flow of oxygen during your long international travel time. But no worries; I've got just the tools to fix them."

"Bigger airholes?" She sighed. "Seriously?"

"It's true that you have a mind for stealth. But are you claiming to be a scientific expert as well? Even if I'm wrong—which, let's be clear, I'm not— what would it hurt to get more air? It's good for your skin!"

"True, true," she admitted, warming up to the idea. "But listen, fish. Express airmail pickup happens in exactly nine minutes. It's the last one of the day. If I miss it, I won't be delivered to the Mew-seum tomorrow."

"Oh, you'll be there tonight," Oscar assured her, "with a glowing complexion." He turned to P.U.G. "Carry this crate parallel to the ground at a speed of two miles per hour. Gently set it down in the middle of the porch." The loyal robo-dog obeyed. "Ophelia, make yourself comfortable inside the crate, and I'll drill the airholes just a bit bigger. You'll be breathing easy the whole way to Paris."

Seven minutes to parcel pickup.

She collapsed in the spa chair, applied a variety of fancy conditioners to her fur, and placed cucumber slices over her eyes.

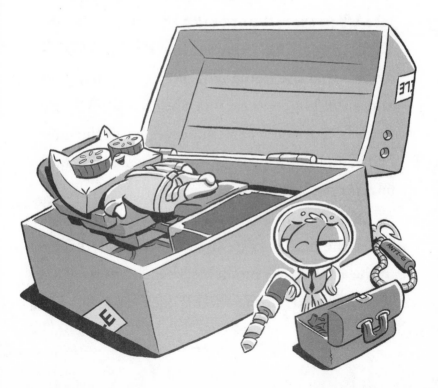

"Whatever you do, fish, try not to make too much noise. I'm going to have a nap now. And please keep your bulgy little eyes on the lookout for anything suspicious before I get picked up."

Oscar saluted her and sealed the travel crate shut.

Four minutes.

Even with Oscar's construction ruckus, Ophelia somehow managed to relax. She took a deep breath and visualized Pierre's surprised face when *she* was announced the winner of the Fifth Annual FFBI Competition. He should know by now that she would win *every* small challenge and *every* big competition. She would set world records! She would cement her legacy as the most brilliant, best-dressed, most epic, world-class cat burglar of all time!

Oscar's drill stopped. Right on time, Ophelia heard the mail carrier, then felt the crate lift up in the air. In a few moments, she felt bumps. This wasn't her first time in the back of a delivery truck.

After about thirty minutes, Ophelia could
tell from the noises outside that she was at the
airport. Soon, the engine of the express airmail
plane rumbled beneath her. She was on her way.

She smiled. The grand plan for her Paris heist and continued cat burglary fame and fortune was coming together.

Suddenly, a rather large jolt displaced the cucumber slices over her eyes.

Incredibly, the face of Oscar Fishgerald Gold, inventor number seventeen, was *one inch from hers*. His massive grin was (freakishly) magnified by his portable tank.

"What?! Why? How did you possibly get in here?" she sputtered. But it didn't take her long to figure out how he'd done it. The airholes he'd drilled were now ever-so-slightly bigger than Oscar's S.P.I.T. *Sneaky fish!*

"You won't even believe how this happened," he exclaimed.

Her reply was strangled. "Try me."

"Well, as I was making the airhole adjustments, the mail carrier pulled up. I didn't want her to ask any questions, so I grabbed my lab kit and a small travel bag and implemented a rather useful recent invention—my antigravity grappling hook—to pull me right in. I guess that means I'm going to Paris with you after all!"

The fish had tricked her! The crate's airholes had been fine before. Ophelia was furious. She didn't like being duped, and she didn't want a fish distraction. "Oscar, don't talk. Once we arrive inside the Mew-seum, you will *stay* in this crate and wait until I have the diamond."

After several hours of silence, Oscar interrupted. "If I may, could we please just talk for

fifteen seconds about my Global Positioning System? Indeed, the GPS is telling me that there's a teensy problem with the trajectory of our flight path."

Even though he was already proving himself as a total, royal, fin-tastic pain in the butt, Ophelia reminded herself that the fish was supersmart. Also, she appreciated his manners. "Okay. You have fifteen seconds. What's the teensy problem?"

So there they were. One stowaway fish-out-of-water and one (fabulous) cat—both headed toward a tiny, cold peninsula on the edge of the sea.

"The first rule of cat burglar club: You do not talk about cat burglar club. The second rule of cat burglar club: If you have to talk about it, don't do it around any finned creature."

—Ophelia von Hairball V

7

A SERIES OF
UN-FUR-TUNATE EVENTS

REMAINING

Is it just me"—Ophelia raised her eyebrows wryly—"or should we be full-on panicking right now?"

"No, no! Much too early to panic," Oscar replied. "Let's just think. Wasn't our plan to be delivered directly to the Belle Mew-seum?"

"That was *my* plan," Ophelia retorted. "I'm not thrilled with this new turn of events. And let's

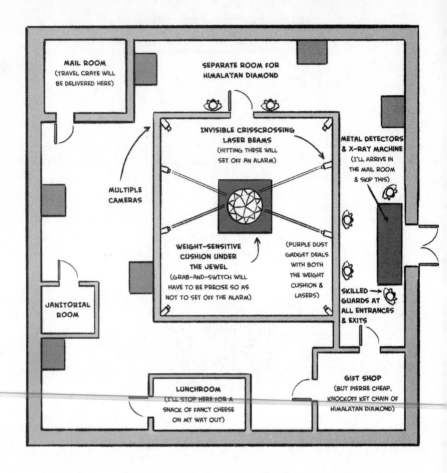

just be real: It's entirely your fault. You were supposed to be my lookout!"

Oscar ignored her. "I read somewhere that one of your mottos is *Be ready to pivot.* Is that not true? Because you seem to be focusing on what's wrong and not on finding a solution."

The cat's eyes narrowed. "There are limits

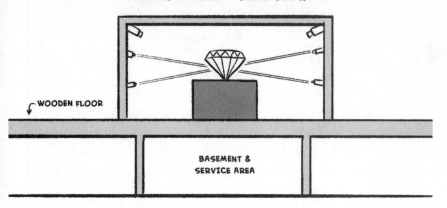

WOODEN FLOOR

BASEMENT &
SERVICE AREA

to my flexibility, fish. I really need to be delivered *inside* the Mew-seum so I can bypass their entrance security. Look for yourself!"

"Hmmm," the inventor agreed, "direct delivery would have been ideal . . . and Norway is quite a long ways from Paris." Oscar tilted his head and looked at her. "But what's plan B? I know your brain is already figuring out a plan B."

Ophelia's brain was moving a mile a minute. "We need to get us—in this crate—out of this plane. Are we anywhere close to Paris?"

"Yes." He pointed to the water churning around inside his S.P.I.T. "There's turbulence; that means wind. Still, I can land us near Paris with a bit of clever engineering . . . if we get out now."

Inside the travel crate, the pair was being tossed around like a ball of yarn in the paws of a street cat. "My plan requires speed," Oscar said, checking his GPS.

"Do tell."

"I'm going to open the plane's emergency hatch. This travel crate will be released into the air . . . along with all the other mail in the plane."

Without further ado, Oscar poked Ophelia's back-scratcher out of the crate and pulled the lever that opened the plane's emergency hatch.

"Get ready for some

WIIINNNDD!"

"Umm . . . EEEeeee!" As the crate left the plane, Ophelia tried to control her screech. "Did we think this through? Did you happen to invent a Jetpack gadget to attach to this crate? Because I'm not so happy about the *plummeting-through-the-air* part of this plan! Or the *crate-smashing-into-the-earth-at-high-speed* part of the plan. And the *cat-and-fish-SPLATTERING-EVERYWHERE* ending to this plan!"

"Oh, don't worry," Oscar assured her over the wind. "There will be no splattering today! We're going to maneuver this crate quite gently right into the heart of the city!"

A jolt of fear traveled from the tips of Ophelia's well-groomed ears to the bottoms of her well-proportioned paws. "'Maneuver'? We're in a crate! In the sky! And we're dropping, Oscar," she yelled. "We're dropping *fast!*"

"Affirmative." He checked his GPS. "We have approximately sixty-five seconds to construct our parachute."

"Don't just stand there, feline! Thirty seconds until I pop the top of this travel crate open and we test our chute. And when the top comes off, *everything* in here is going to fly out. Whatever you absolutely need, put inside the trunk. I'll bolt it down."

Very quickly, Ophelia put her necessities, plus a few of her favorite possessions, into the trunk. Oscar shoved in a few gadgets and his suitcase and screwed the top shut. He bolted the trunk down, then attached ropes to the four corners of the Persian carpet and secured them to the floor.

"Ta-da! The trunk is shut tight and our parachute is ready. Fifteen seconds until I take the lid off this travel crate," Oscar yelled over the roar of turbulence. "The air will catch underneath the carpet and we'll float—like a fabulous feather boa—to Paris. Hold on to something! And *whatever* you do, don't let go."

"Not letting go!" Ophelia assured him, and dug her strong claws into the side of the crate. She made a mental note to thank the manicurist who kept her nails sharp and strong.

Like an astronaut tethered to a spaceship, Oscar attached his S.P.I.T. to the trunk and positioned himself to pop the top off the travel crate. "Three, two, one . . ." With shark-like speed, he freed the four corners of the lid.

Ophelia held her breath as the crate top spun off into the atmosphere (along with several priceless items).

She waited to hear the *POP!* of the rug snapping open to slow them down . . . but nothing happened. The carpet remained flat. The pair continued to drop toward the earth.

"So, fish, when do we start floating like that feather boa you promised? Exactly when is this parachute going to start working?" Ophelia yelled. But the fear in Oscar's bulgy eyes said it all. *It should have already started to work.*

They say cats have nine lives. Ophelia closed her eyes and hoped she had at least one left.

"There will be times in life that aren't fun.
Try not to have too many of those."

—Ophelia von Hairball V

8

NOT A-MEWS-ED

REMAINING

For a few very looong seconds, Oscar and Ophelia stared at each other, waiting for a gust of air to lift their makeshift parachute and slow the travel crate. But the heavy rug stayed stuck, flat to the crate's floor. Their high-speed plummet toward the earth continued. A lifetime of heists flashed before Ophelia's eyes; she'd come too far and worked too hard to let Pierre win now. Her last moments would not be in a travel crate with a random fish inventor. "Let's do this!" Ophelia shouted at Oscar. "Let's make this parachute inflate and get to Paris!"

"I can't understand why it's stuck!" he said, a bit panicked.

"This would be a *very* good moment to impress me with your genius mind," Ophelia ordered.

Still tethered, Oscar wiggled himself to the middle of the crate. With all his might, he wedged his fin under the side of the rug and lifted it to look.

"Oh dear," he said. "There's something incredibly sticky under here. And glossy." He peered closer and sniffed. "It's claw polish!" He raised an eyebrow. "And if my identification skills are as good as I think, I'd say it's Sphynx Scarlet claw polish that's sticking our parachute to the floor. Did you really need Sphynx Scarlet for a diamond heist?"

"We're plummeting toward the earth with no parachute. Is there really time for so much judgment?" Ophelia inquired.

"No worries! We've got this." Oscar wiggled himself under the carpet and pulled the rug with all his might. For a moment, the polish held the rug like glue. Finally, it came unstuck with a SMACK! "Come on, parachute! Come ON!"

WHOOSH! The wind caught under the rug. There was a hard jerk, and their descent toward the earth began to slow. Relief washed over the cat. "It's working!"

"But of course," Oscar retorted. He surveyed the ground below. "Hmmm. Looks like the brief delay set us off course a bit. The good news is that we're not too far from Paris. The bad news? We might land in the water."

Ophelia froze. Besides Pierre, pugs, and poodles, water was her greatest enemy.

"Don't fret! I see a ship down there," Oscar yelled. "I'm going to try to steer this thing. With any luck, we'll land on it. Brace yourself!"

Ophelia curled up into a ball in the corner and prepared for a harsh landing.

Closer and closer they drifted, as Oscar chattered away, hoping to impress Ophelia. "Did you know the first scientist to measure speed as distance over time was Galileo? Now *there* was an interesting chap. He sketched several inventions, including a candle-and-mirror combo, an automatic tomato picker, a pocket comb that doubled as a sort of fork, and a ballpoint pen. . . ."

"Do you mind zipping it, fin-boy? If I die, I'd like to hear the wind rushing through my glorious fur and not you nattering on about tomatoes. Just worry about where we're going!"

"I am a gold-star navigator," Oscar assured her. "Definitely the right fish for this job. Here we go!" They landed with a small *thud.*

"Are you okay?" the fish asked as he brushed himself off.

"I seem to be," Ophelia answered, happy to be alive. "At least we didn't hit the water." She smoothed her fur in relief. "I'm really going to need some spa time later."

Oscar hopped up and looked over the edge of the crate, surveying their location. "All right then! I'm going to recommend that you hold your nose," Oscar warned. "It's too bad you don't have a S.P.I.T. It shields me from . . . THE SMELL!"

When Ophelia stood up and took a deep breath, the stench hit her like a rotten wave. It was like all the very worst odors were trapped together, then magnified and heated.

"I'm almost certain," Oscar said, "that I know where we are, and it's in the English Channel near France's shoreline. Just a short two hour and forty-five minute train ride to the center of Paris."

Ophelia nodded. They could easily get to the Mew-seum before closing time.

Oscar wasn't done. "Unfortunately we may, in fact, be on, um, a garbage barge, and I'm not entirely sure how we're going to actually *get* to the shoreline."

"A-a-a gar ... GARBAGE BARGE?"

"At least we're close to Paris!" he assured her. "Imagine if we'd stayed on that plane and landed in Norway! Although, I've always wanted to swim in the fjords."

"Double ugh." Ophelia plugged her nose and gingerly stepped out of the crate. Their surroundings were grim. Heaps of moldy, rotten food, piles of old gym socks, cushions from decrepit couches, and a variety of unidentified horrors were all around them.

"Hey ... what are those evil-looking creatures?" Oscar's voice shook. "They look very hungry."

"They're excessively large rats." Ophelia did a halfhearted hiss in their direction, and they scattered. "Thankfully, they're scared of me." Ophelia turned back to Oscar. "Depending on your next moves, I may or may not hand you over to them. But first, fish-face, what I'd like to know is HOW our destination changed from Paris to Norway. Please help me flip this crate." Ophelia had a theory about how it might have happened. (It involved her shady cousin.)

Turning the crate over confirmed her suspicions—the address had been changed. And under the packing tape was Pierre's calling card.

"See? I made the Paris address tag for this travel crate myself, and this new address must have been added *after* I was inside. Just imagine how helpful you could have been if you'd been *outside* the crate making sure the pickup was smooth rather than sneaking into it! Your insistence on being a stowaway cost us hours of time." She stuck her nose in the air. "Not to mention the lasting damage to my delicate psyche. I'll need aromatherapy for years."

Oscar cocked an eyebrow. "Let's not dwell on the past. According to my calculations, this garbage barge is precisely 8.047 kilometers—five miles—from shore. From there, Paris and the Mew-seum are a short train ride away." He smiled. "Remember the custom scuba suit? We could swim to shore!"

"NO!" She shook her head. "Fur real, it would take me three *years* to swim from here to shore! I hate the water, and I detest swimming. Are you telling me that supersmart brain of yours can't formulate any better plan than putting my body into the water?" Her voice rose with dramatic exasperation. "Fish, please! We're on a boat! Get us to shore! As dry as possible!"

Oscar tapped his fin to his forehead in deep thought. "Even if I built a top-notch engine, this barge is too big to move quickly. But there *is* another scenario that will allow us to get to the Belle Mew-seum before closing today. I predict that you won't like it, though."

"Whatever your plan is, it's better than being stuck on a garbage barge, and it's better than swimming. Do what you need to do!"

"No complaining?" Oscar asked.

"No. None!" she solemnly declared. (He didn't notice her paws were crossed.)

"Okay. Let's see which of our possessions—"

"*My* possessions."

"You're so nitpicky! Let's see which of YOUR possessions made it through the crash landing."

Oscar's head drooped. "Yes. It's totally ruined." The grab-and-switch device he'd so carefully constructed had been jolted with the impact of their landing. "On the bright side," he said, "the gold-button-tornado feature was destroyed. Can you imagine the mess if we had accidentally triggered that on this garbage barge?"

"That's the bright side?!" Ophelia hissed.

Oscar sighed and wiped the fine, purple powder particles off his S.P.I.T. "Such a fin-tastic plan up in smoke!"

"They say humility is the key.
Thankfully, I can pick any lock."

—Ophelia von Hairball V

9

SEA YOU LATER

Ophelia shook the purple dust from her fur and looked at her fish companion. "You resemble a famous little egg-shaped jewel I once stole," she remarked wryly.

Oscar seemed flustered. "Ugh! Without that grab-and-switch gadget, once we find a way inside the Mew-seum, we'll need an entirely new plan to steal the diamond!"

"Indeed." His use of *we* grated on Ophelia, but he looked so silly trying to rid himself of his dusty purple film that she resisted the urge to correct him.

"How about you plot and find a new way to get into the Mew-seum and take the jewel," Oscar suggested, "and I'll make us a worthy sea vessel!"

For the next hour, Oscar worked. Piece by piece, he destroyed the luxury travel crate and almost everything in it. As some of her priceless items were transformed into a boat, Ophelia cringed. But true to her word, she didn't complain.

"Almost done. Please go fetch—I mean *find*—ten plastic milk jugs," he ordered, beads of sweat forming on his fins. "I also need some metal scraps. You might have to dig for those. . . ."

"But my manicure!" Ophelia protested.

"Would you like to stay here forever?" As he pried the last of the travel crate's boards apart, Oscar suddenly stopped. "Ophelia! Take a look at this!" He held up a minuscule metal disk the size of a pencil eraser.

"Is that what I think it is?" Ophelia looked at the inventor, but she already knew the answer.

"Yes. I fear, dear cat, that this is a rather sophisticated tracking device. It's amazing technology—the smallest I've ever seen. It seems as if your cousin did more than just switch the address on your travel crate. He's also keeping a close eye on where we are."

Ophelia was confused and examined the metal disk more closely. "That is not Pierre's," she declared. "It's too well constructed. Too polished. Pierre uses cheap tracking devices. He buys them in bulk."

"But who else would be tracking you?" Oscar didn't wait for her guess. "Let's look for a clue inside this thing." He used a small paper clip from a nearby pile of rubble to pry it open.

Ophelia wasn't amused, either. It dawned on her that she was now evading both Pierre *and* the Central Canine Intelligence Agency.

Oscar closed the bug back up and put it in a small chunk of moldy bread. He threw it up in the air and a humongous seagull swooped down to grab it. "That'll throw the CCIA off for a while. They really would like nothing more than to nab you, Ophelia. Imagine those dogs being able to say they caught you, the top cat burglar in the world!"

Ophelia didn't want to think about it.

"Back to work!"

Before too long, Oscar had finished his nautical masterpiece.

Ophelia plucked her special-ops handbag from the pile of things that Oscar hadn't hacked to pieces.

"That bag looks too big," Oscar told her. "Can you leave it here?"

"This," she stated with conviction, "is an absolute necessity. I need it. In fact, I never go on a heist without it. My grandma gave it to me."

Oscar nodded. "You're a high-maintenance cat," he said matter-of-factly. "And I know you don't know it yet, but even though you are really legendary on your own, you might actually learn to love having a great inventor at your side!"

Ophelia rolled her eyes.

"In any case, you shouldn't have a bag that big on *any* heist. When we're home, I'll construct you something tiny but beautiful—a compact masterpiece to match any outfit!"

"This bag might be large, but it's filled with very lovely compartments. And you never know what you might need!" She spotted Oscar's gravity-defying grappling hook on the ground and popped it in her bag. It could come in handy.

The fish tapped his fin. "I think you're being stubborn. Isn't there always room for improveme—" Oscar stopped talking when the massive seagull swooped back around, looked at Oscar, and greedily licked its lips.

"You seem to be a good snack option." Ophelia chuckled.

One paw at a time, Ophelia tentatively tested out the makeshift transportation. "Are you sure we won't sink in this?"

"Positive."

"If I get soggy . . ."

"Trust me," Oscar assured her. "I've sailed every sea on the map and some that *aren't* on the map. I'll keep you dry."

They cruised across the water toward Paris at high speed, and thanks to the inventor's solid ship design, Ophelia, as promised, didn't get wet.

When they got to France's shoreline, the fish captain maneuvered them to a small dock, where he anchored and tied their boat. "Do you think Pierre's watching for us?"

"Probably," Ophelia replied. "Not to mention the CCIA." She sighed. "There are a lot of enemies to keep track of. Just try to stay low."

"I'm not really very good at slinking," he admitted. "But I've been practicing! I want to make you proud."

They moved slowly and carefully. The short hike from the dock to the train station was uneventful.

The entire way, Ophelia was trying to decide how to tell Oscar that it was time for him to go home. Admittedly, the fish had been quite useful. Still, a paw-rtner would undoubtedly get in her way.

As they approached the train station, Ophelia cleared her throat and turned to her theater training to help her find (and keep) a just-right, wide whisker-to-whisker smile on her face.

PROCHAIN ARRÊT, **PARIS.**

"Ah! They're announcing my train. Thank you so very much, Oscar F. Gold. You're quite an inventor. And there's a top-notch burglar somewhere in the FFBI who will find you very helpful! I've got to hurry now. You'll get your own ride home?"

"Home?" The fish looked confused. "Oh no, no, no. I'm coming with you! This is, by far, the most exciting thing that's ever happened to me. It's been my dream to work with you! I've never been so happy!"

Ophelia knew there was no way she could pull off an almost-impossible heist *and* babysit this awkward, stowaway fan-fish. She cleared her throat and shifted her approach from polite to pointed. "While I appreciate your enthusiasm, there's ZERO chance you're staying with me. Pierre is already a step ahead. And who knows what's happening with the crazy canines? From here, I shall take the train to Paris, steal the diamond, then get to Brussels to claim my first-place prize in the FFBI Purr-fect Heist Competition before the deadline."

Oscar's eyes widened in disbelief, but the cat stood her ground. "Here's some money. Fly first class! Put your fins up and relax! Then, when you're home, make sure to say hello to MEW for me. Oh, and do me a favor: Let her know I've been polite and kind to you. Au revoir! Wish me luck!"

Ophelia waved, then jumped onto the train to Paris and the Belle Mew-seum.

She didn't look back.

She should have.

"The only thing to fear is fear itself . . . or a jerk-face feline with too much fur above his eyes."

—Ophelia von Hairball V

10

PLANS FUR-LORN

Paris is known for being fashion fur-ward, and Ophelia was absolutely ready for it. With just a few minor wardrobe adjustments, she was almost invisible among the chic train station crowds in rush-hour traffic.

She found a seat in the train car, grabbed a newspaper, and settled in to look natural

(naturally amazing, that is). She hid her Mew-seum map inside the paper so no one could see it.

Across from her, a dog stranger smiled. Though she couldn't place him, he looked a bit fur-miliar. Every instinct told her to be on high alert. "*Nouveau á Paris?*" the stranger inquired. Although she was fluent in French (and ten other languages), Ophelia didn't want to encourage conversation, so she smiled and shrugged, pretending not to understand.

With a keen eye, she peered around the train. Two more dogs were seated close to her, looking bored—almost as if they were *pretending* to be bored. Her whiskers twitched with suspicion.

The stranger tried again—this time in English. "Have you visited Paris before?"

Ophelia needed to know if she was dealing with the CCIA. She remembered MEW had told her that the CCIA liked to have their logo on everything.

"Achoo! *Achoo!!* ACHOO!!!" She fake-sneezed three times—each louder than the last. "Pardon me!" she exclaimed. "Oh my! Would you be so kind as to lend me your handkerchief?"

There was a flicker of hesitation, and Ophelia could see the stranger squirm. Unless he wanted to be very rude, he had no choice but to pass his handkerchief over. "*Mais oui!* But of course!"

Though the flustered dog tried to crumple it, she could clearly see the CCIA symbol embossed in the bottom-right corner.

Clever canines. Ophelia was surprised that the CCIA dogs had found her. She had hoped they'd still be following the seagull that chomped their tracking device. MEW was right—this organization was more dangerous to the FFBI than she'd first thought.

Ophelia knew the CCIA would need to catch her red-pawed in order to take her into custody. And if that happened, her reputation as an elite burglar would be ruined. She would have to stay on high alert.

"Thank you so much," she said, returning the handkerchief. She didn't let on that she'd seen the CCIA symbol. "And no. *Je ne parlez paws fran-sez.*" She put her head back into her newspaper.

When the train arrived in the city, Ophelia took every possible precaution to lose the CCIA dogs following her. She climbed trees, went in and out of random buildings, and changed outfits several times until she was certain they were no longer on her tail.

Aware that her time was running short, she hurried over the cobblestone streets. As she made her way to the famous Belle Mew-seum, she recognized many of the quaint stores. It had been ages since she'd been to Paris. Ophelia wondered if she might be able to sneak in some hat shopping after the heist.

Finally, in front of her target building, Ophelia stood tall, ready for action. She soaked in the white marble, lush gardens, and well-dressed visitors. The Mew-seum was much more grandiose in person. Among all the luxury, Ophelia could almost smell sweet victory . . . but realized the delicious scents were coming from the bakery across the street. She strolled over and took a seat at an outdoor table.

Since the Mew-seum closed in an hour, Ophelia only had a few minutes for reconnaissance. With such high security at the front doors, she wondered if there was, perhaps, another way to get into—and out of—the Mew-seum.

Through binoculars (that were ever-so-smartly disguised as a camera), Ophelia watched carefully as a steady stream of people entered and exited the Mew-seum through the front door. The building also had a side emergency exit, and

there looked to be a rooftop atrium, but without more time to plan, she'd have to risk going in and out through the front entrance like everyone else.

Although she knew a great many FFBI agents who liked to fly by the seat of their pants, it wasn't Ophelia's favorite way to work. Still, she reminded herself that she'd pulled off a few spur-of-the-moment heists in the past. A waiter approached.

"Bonjour. I'm Simon. I'll be serving you today."

"One of your deliciously decadent chocolate croissants, please, with butter. And a tea with milk. I'm in a bit of a hurry."

"Of course."

Simon quickly returned to her table with the flaky treat. In the small dish of butter was the FFBI symbol.

I CAN'T TELL FOR SURE...

BUT THAT LITTERBUG EITHER HAS A **MASSIVE CATERPILLAR** STUCK TO THE TOP OF HIS NOSE...

OR THAT'S THE MOST **IMPRESSIVE UNIBROW** I'VE EVER SEEN.

"Ophelia! I'm FFBI," Simon whispered. "Not as high ranking as you, of course, but I'm a big fan. Let me know how I can help!"

"I'm competing in the Purr-fect Heist Competition right now. Looks like someone wants to stop me. Do you know if the diamond has been stolen yet?" Ophelia asked. She feared that another burglar—worst of all Pierre—had already nabbed it.

Simon nodded. "I've seen some action across the street," he said, "but as far as I know, the jewel is still there. It's ready for you to pluck!" He smiled. "Do check the back room of my bakery before you go. There's a fresh disguise for you there. And your snack is on the house today. Good luck."

"Merci!" Grateful for the unexpected help, she exited the patio and found her way through the bakery's kitchen. On a hook, a rather bold disguise awaited her. It took several minutes, but with (a LOT of) hair spray, a bandanna, some very real-looking facial hair, and some studded black leather, Ophelia transformed from a raving beauty into a radical biker cat.

The disguise had more hair than she normally liked, but Ophelia decided it would serve its purpose very well. Both Pierre and the CCIA would be looking for a glamorous tourist, and she looked nothing like the sleek, sophisticated cat on the wanted poster she'd seen outside the bakery.

With bold and beautiful confidence, Ophelia went into her character just like every great actor and stomped across the street to the Belle Mewseum, ready to take on any obstacle to get the Himalayan diamond!

"Even when I'm alone, I'm not lonely. Because inside me is a rough-and-tumble cowgirl. And a sparkling superstar. And a mad scientist. And every other persona I can imagine."

—Ophelia von Hairball V

11

MEW, MEW, MEW-SEUM

HOURS MINUTES

16 21

REMAINING

Even though the Belle Mew-seum was crowded, Ophelia wished she could roam around the building as a tourist and take in all the magnificent art. The entrance security was a gauntlet of guards and metal detectors. "Hello." Ophelia nodded, trying a casual smile through her new facial hair. The fake mustache tickled her nose.

The crabby-looking guard addressed her in English. "Head on through there," she said.

This was the tricky part. Ophelia did NOT want her handbag to go through the X-ray machine. "I've got an old-fashioned camera in here with unexposed film," Ophelia cautioned. "The machine might damage it. Do you mind hand-searching my bag instead?"

"Okay," the guard muttered, annoyed. "Give me your bag. Step through the machine."

These were the moments that mattered. Ophelia's heart beat like a drum.

The guard opened Ophelia's handbag and removed a few things. Right away, she honed in on a bejeweled nail file. Nervous, Ophelia realized it was possible the guard might have seen it on the news—Ophelia had recently "acquired" it from a private collection in Hawaii.

"Supercute. Doesn't really look like your style, though," the guard challenged.

A small fib was in order. "It's a souvenir for my niece."

The guard smiled. "Ah! I bought my daughter

one just like this yesterday at the two-cent store."

It took all her might, but Ophelia held back an eye roll. *That nail file is worth a lot more than two cents! It's worth a small castle!*

"I hope your niece loves it."

"Why, thank you," Ophelia said. "It will be cat-astrophic if she doesn't." Thankfully, the guard didn't dig any deeper in her bag to find the grappling hook or other, suspicious knick-knacks.

"Okay. Put all this junk back in your bag. Please note the Mew-seum closes in just under an hour."

Beneath her beard, Ophelia's smile was huge. *Time for action.*

Now that she was past security, she had to make a few things happen:

- Find an object the same weight as the diamond.
- Get into the Himalayan diamond room and make everyone else leave.

- Expose the laser beams and get to the gem's podium without setting off an alarm.
- Perform the grab-and-switch maneuver.
- Stroll (with the diamond) out the front door.

Ophelia remembered that her grab-and-switch object needed to be 3,501.17 carats, or approximately 24.7 ounces—just about the weight of two soup cans. Thankfully the Mew-seum had many interesting trinkets—almost as many as she had in her very own secret lair! Even though she was feeling the stress of the challenge, Ophelia knew her creativity and inventive nature would help her.

The Egyptian exhibit looked like it had smaller items that would be fairly easy for her to pilfer. As she admired all the gold, the wall monitor in front of her flickered.

Was it possible that someone was trying to communicate with her through the screen? She shook her head and blinked a few times. Maybe she'd breathed in too many stinky fumes on the garbage barge.

OSCAR? OSCAR?! Somehow, the fish was intercepting the signals and sending his own messages. She put her wireless earpiece in and tuned in to the FFBI-approved channel.

Nobody else seemed to notice Oscar's fish-face on the monitor.

"Cheers, Ophelia! You can talk back to me through the microphone in your earpiece. It's a secure channel."

She was fuming. How dare he risk compromising her cover? She hissed into her watch, "Do you even want to know what I'll do to you if I don't win this competition because of your tomfishery?!"

"Oh, relax," Oscar replied. "I've done this before."

"Indeed! Also, be aware of the time! There are thirty-five minutes left. Please keep your earpiece in so I can communicate with you. And while you're doing the heist, I'm going to enjoy another delicious bite from this bakery and soak in some of the gorgeous fashions here in Paris. I'm sure it will inspire some new outfit ideas. Let me know if you need anything!"

Ophelia sighed and removed her earpiece. She was *so close* to the diamond and her prize—and yet so very far. What she needed was a new grand plan—one as unexpected as she was.

"Whenever and wherever you can in life, make a big splash. But not in actual water."

—Ophelia von Hairball V

12

CAT-CH ME IF YOU CAN

HOURS | MINUTES
15 | **29**
REMAINING

ood afternoon, guests!" A voice came over the intercom. "It is now four thirty." Ophelia's time was running out! "The Mew-seum will close in thirty minutes. Also . . . can we get a few mops to the front of the insect displays, please?"

Ophelia watched a janitor go by with his mop. Of course! A rather risky idea started to take shape. With all the rushing and panic, Ophelia almost lost sight of one of the most important cat burglary secrets of all time: Your biggest obstacle might also be the best part of your plan.

Placing her earpiece back into her ear, she waded through the crowds toward the bathroom to equip a brand-new disguise.

Twice, she thought she spotted some suspicious-looking dogs, but there was no time to investigate. She had just under thirty minutes until closing time! Ophelia knew she needed every single second.

"Oscar," Ophelia whispered into her watch. There was silence on the other end. "Oscar, expect to hear a few alarms and sirens soon, but don't panic. I've got a plan. Keep your bulgy eyes peeled for Pierre or any of those CCIA mutts. I haven't seen them yet, but I've got a feeling they could be here."

She didn't wait for the fish to reply. Instead, she traded her biker disguise for a janitor outfit and a mop and double-checked her special-ops handbag. She had everything she needed.

Adrenaline surged from the tip of her tail to her claws. She was so close to winning!

With only fifteen minutes left before the staff cleared everyone out of the Mew-seum, Ophelia confidently walked right past security and entered the gem room, where the Himalayan diamond sparkled brilliantly on its pedestal. Nobody questioned when she set up a CLOSED FOR CLEANING sign.

Ophelia knew the next few moments would either put her in the hiss-tory books or behind bars. The clock was ticking.

She shooed several people out of the room. When she was finally alone, Ophelia made her bold move. With a deep breath, she pounced through the array of invisible lasers directly to the pedestal where the precious gem sparkled. As she anticipated, the titanium bars shot up to encase her with a loud *BOOM*! It was just like Oscar had warned! She was a prisoner—with the beloved Himalayan diamond.

Just like she wanted.

In her handbag, Ophelia had the special grappling hook Oscar made her, plus the file, which would serve as a dandy glass cutter of sorts. All she needed to do was attach the grappling hook to the chandelier, zip herself up, cut through the atrium window, and escape!

But before she could reach for the hook that would take her up to the ceiling, she heard a bark that made her fur prickle.

"Well, well. If it isn't the infamous cat burglar, Ophelia von Hairball V. We can get to know each other later—once you're in CCIA custody. For now, let me just say that there's no escape for you. This room is surrounded by agents who are very excited to be part of your arrest."

AND IF YOU TAKE A PEEK UP **ABOVE,**

IN CASE YOU'D PLANNED A **WOOF-TOP ESCAPE,**

YOU'LL SEE THAT OUR **AGENTS** ARE WAITING.

A slow, sly grin spread across the cat burglar's face, and she looked toward her adversary. His face was hidden by shadows. "Well, doggone it! I guess you've caught me then." Her tail twitched, and, as if defeated, she sat down, mop in paw. Ophelia kept talking as she reached into her special-ops handbag, searching for her diamond-encrusted nail file and dental floss. Without looking down, she wrapped the floss around the nail file over and over, then tied dozens of knots to secure the file to the mop head. In no time, the file was solidly attached. "While I admire your purr-sistence and the loyalty to your cause, I'll never understand why your organization feels the need to be constantly barking up our trees. We're harmless. Members of the FFBI demonstrate superior skills, then return our spoils. Cat burglary is a very old and respected art form."

The CCIA agent listened intently to Ophelia, occasionally panting. He was oblivious to the work she was doing with the mop and the file. When he spoke, he seemed pleased with himself. "What you and the FFBI do is constantly break rules. The CCIA must maintain paw and order at all costs! It is our one and only mandate. Our motto! And now we'll finally have you behind bars!"

"Well, live and let live is what I always say." Ophelia smiled and stood up to look him in the eyes. "I'm all for paw and order, sir," she stated, "but the thing is, I've got a very important competition to win today."

NEXT, USING ALL HER MIGHT AND HER DIAMOND-TIPPED MOP,

SHE CUT A BEAUTIFUL CIRCLE THROUGH THE **WOODEN FLOORBOARDS.**

SAW SAW SAW

STOMP!

CRACK!

BAM! OPHELIA AND THE DIAMOND DROPPED TO THE BASEMENT.

She'd outwitted the silly dogs! Above her, Ophelia could hear the chaos and mayhem. There was yelling and the thudding of paws and feet as everyone ran around, panicked by the alarm bells she'd set off. Ophelia wasn't home free yet. She knew she had to keep her cool. It wouldn't take the guards too long to realize what had happened.

Carefully, Ophelia freed her file from the mop head. Then she grabbed the massive gem.

There was only one other annoying detail to worry about. She still had to get the fish. "Oscar!" she said into her microphone. "I got it! And I have a very good story for you. It involves dogs and the woof. I mean the *roof.* Stay where you are. I'm coming to get you."

The Mew-seum's alarm was still blaring as she ditched her disguise and crawled through an air vent that led to the main floor. Quickly (but with an appropriate amount of elegance), she got lost in the mass of people exiting the building.

Out of the corner of her eye, she saw a group of frustrated CCIA members sniffing the crowds. Head lowered, she continued to the door. Just before the entire Mew-seum was locked down, she vanished.

She couldn't help but strut a bit as she walked toward the bakery where Oscar was waiting. It was a lot of excitement for one day! She felt exhilarated and exhausted.

Her plan was to shop for a new hat, then head to Brussels and claim her prize. After that, maybe she'd treat herself to a fancy spa where she could unwind. But first, she'd collect her pesky inventor and gloat about the diamond before she (once again) sent him packing.

Near the bakery, she looked for the fish. Suddenly, her stomach sank like an anchor.

Pierre! In one hand, he held a cookie. In the other, he held a small plastic bag. As Ophelia got

closer, she confirmed that the little bag had a small fish inventor inside—and from the amount of frantic bubbles he was churning up, he was obviously distressed.

"There are plenty of fish in the sea. And that's where they should stay."

—Ophelia von Hairball V

13

TIP THE SCALES

HOURS   MINUTES

14   57

REMAINING

Pierre's single eyebrow was larger-than-life, and Ophelia wanted to tell him that his blue satin suit wasn't appropriate for a bakery patio—or anywhere on Earth. Instead, she simply gave him her very best glare.

"Well, hello, cousin! Do take a seat." Pierre oozed smugness. He set the plastic bag on the table but kept it close. Inside, poor Oscar looked terrified.

Ophelia's first instinct was to tell Pierre to flush the fish, and she could keep walking with her diamond. But her insides were sparking with FUR-Y! How dare Pierre steal her inventor?!

Ophelia sat down in angry silence, and Simon the waiter approached the table. If he knew something fishy was going on, he didn't show it. "I do hope you got to view the diamond?" Simon inquired innocently. "There was quite a kerfuffle across the street. . . ."

"I was lucky enough to see the gem," she responded quietly. "It's impressive." She wished she could safely signal Simon to grab the plastic bag and save Oscar, but Ophelia thought that in Pierre's desperation to win the Purr-fect Heist Competition, he might go to extreme measures. Ophelia decided she needed to handle the situation delicately. After taking their snack orders, Simon walked away.

"Cat got your tongue, cousin?" Pierre hissed. "You might win the staring contest, but if you

want your little finned friend back in one piece, I'm going to need that diamond from you." His sneer made Ophelia's stomach churn. "Have anything to say?"

"Like what, Pierre? Like you were too chicken to go get the diamond yourself? So, as usual, you waited for me to do the hard work? You call yourself a cat burglar, but you don't deserve the title."

Pierre's eyes narrowed. Close up, his furrowed brow was menacing. "I do deserve it! I'm as fancy and classy as you are! You're just mad because I outsmarted you this time. You see, once I realized you weren't going to give up, I decided to make it easy on myself."

Ophelia knew what she had to do. "I'll give you the diamond but not the bag."

Her cousin scrunched his face. "Oh! You're so mean! I still don't know why Grandma gave you that bag and me an ugly sweater. Fish for the bag. Fair trade."

Oscar, who had been silent during the negotiations, piped up. "Um . . . slightly embarrassing, but if you don't mind, Pierre, can you please give Ophelia my suitcase as well? I don't have any other clean underwear with me."

Pierre placed Oscar and his small suitcase in the middle of the table. "I don't want your ridiculous inventor or his soggy underwear. For your information, I was just awarded an amazing inventor of my own. His name is Norman."

Ophelia choked down a giggle and suppressed the urge to tell him to get an exterminator and start loving knock-knock jokes. "Pierre, even if you take this diamond from me and win the Purrfect Heist Competition, you'll *never* be the FFBI's number-one cat burglar. Not ever."

He sneered. "Really? For this particular

competition, the FFBI only requires that I get the diamond to their Brussels HQ first. They don't care how it all happens. And once I win *even one* of these big competitions, doubt will be cast on your superiority."

She knew he was right. For a moment, Ophelia seriously pondered the possibility of saying no—of leaving the fish with Pierre. Did she really care if Oscar became sushi? He was her seventeenth inventor after all, and if he disappeared, the FFBI might finally realize that she shouldn't have one. Besides, the fish had brought this on himself. If he hadn't stowed away in her travel crate, he wouldn't have ended up trapped in a plastic bag!

But a couple of thoughts swirled around in Ophelia's mind. *If Oscar hadn't come along, I might be in Norway! If Oscar hadn't built that boat, I might have been stranded forever . . . on a garbage barge! And if Oscar hadn't transmitted the message about the Mew-seum's new security, I might be in CCIA custody!*

"All right, all right," Ophelia conceded. Reluctantly, she put her special-ops handbag on the table. "My bag for the fish."

Pierre smirked. "I guess this is good-bye, then. To celebrate *me* getting the diamond, I'm throwing myself a very fancy party on my yacht tonight at the Port of Le Havre," he bragged. "Then, as I sleep, my captain will transport me to Brussels. I'll arrive just in time—and well rested—to give my victory speech!" He frowned and his eyebrow formed a V. "I was thinking about mentioning you but decided against it." He gave them a wave. "It's been a pleasure doing business with you."

Ophelia's whiskers twitched as her archrival trotted off. She quickly freed the tiny inventor from his small plastic prison.

Oscar straightened his collar. "Well done! Thank you for making the trade. I have to say, when that rascal scooped me up, I thought I was shark bait. The odds of you trading the Himalayan diamond for me seemed minuscule. I'm so glad I was wrong!"

"Zip it, fish." Ophelia looked deep into his bulgy eyes. *"Tell me you are still carrying that ridiculous scuba suit you made.* Also, give me assurances that it's scientifically guaranteed to be COMPLETELY waterproof."

"Well, yes. Of course I brought it. Take a look for yourself!" He popped open his suitcase and *two* matching scuba suits emerged. "I actually made two, so we can be a team. Do you just love

the logo? O²! Oscar and Ophelia! Get it? We have a team code name!"

Ophelia shook her head. "You're a fish! You don't need a scuba suit!"

Oscar blinked and looked offended. "*Obviously.* But it's a fashion statement, Ophelia. It shows I'm a team player. Unlike some cats I know."

Ophelia rolled her eyes. "Is mine really waterproof?"

"Of course it's waterproof," he chided. "I told you, I've got the best gadget gills on the planet." He perched his fins on the table and his eyes twinkled. "So are we going swimming together or what?!" Oscar asked.

Ophelia's tail swished. "Indeed we are, smallfry. Pierre said he was on a yacht, right? Your team dream is about to come true. You will assist me in stealing that diamond … again."

"When all hope seems lost, check the last handbag you used. It might still be there."

—Ophelia von Hairball V

14

GOLD-FIN-GER

REMAINING

Oscar's smile was magnified through his S.P.I.T. "Are we really going to steal back the diamond as a team?" They sat together, waiting for Simon to lock up the bakery.

"You bet your gold fins we are," Ophelia vowed. Oscar beamed. "But we're going to have to time this just right. The moment Pierre goes to sleep, we'll have a small window to take back the gem. If we wait too long, his yacht will be gone."

Simon chimed in. "I'll drive you to the Port of Le Havre now."

Oscar checked his clock. "We're really cutting this close. What if we can't find his boat?"

Ophelia nodded. "Trust me, it won't be hard to see Pierre's boat. What I'm worried about is the CCIA. Even if we're careful, Pierre probably hasn't been. I'm sure those dogs have followed him. Simon, do you know a route down to the Port that bypasses the main road?"

"But of course."

As the sun set, Simon dropped the duo off by the water. "Good luck, friends! If you ever need more help—or baked goods—look me up!"

"We owe you," Ophelia told him.

"*Vo-treh coolay la form de la fermay de poms de tear de ma grand-mare!*" Oscar bellowed at him, and waved good-bye.

"You know," Ophelia advised the fish, "you just told him that his butt is the shape of your grandmother's potato farm."

"Oh." He shrugged. "I guess I'll need to come back to Paris again to practice my French."

From the road, Oscar and Ophelia walked down to the dock. They were hidden by large trees and shrubs. Once they got to the water, they changed into their matching scuba suits. The moon was full, and it cast a beautiful light onto the waves. As Ophelia had predicted, Pierre's yacht was a bobbing beacon of tacky, neon lights.

"We'll hide in these bushes," Ophelia told Oscar when she'd scoped out a spot. "Leave your suitcase here; we'll pick it up after. As soon as the fancy lights turn off, it's go time! We need to get the diamond off that boat before it leaves for Brussels!"

"Ow!" Oscar exclaimed, trying to settle into the bush. "It's a fact that foliage and fish don't really go together very well."

"Being out in the field is not always luxurious," Ophelia agreed. "Despite the fact that I always look the face of glamour, I sometimes have to perform purr-fect crimes sans my fur products!"

"I can't even imagine the horror," Oscar teased. "I've never been to a fur salon."

"Shhh! There he is!"

Pierre was out on the bow of his ship, cavorting wildly in his gaudy, striped pajamas.

Ophelia reminded Oscar of the plan she'd devised. "Remember, when we get to the boat, I need to steal my *whole* special-ops bag back."

"Why the whole bag?" he asked. "It'll be easier to swim back with just the diamond. Surely Pierre's already taken out the gem."

"I don't think so," she said. "That handbag isn't easy to get into. There's a heavy-duty lock on the zipper. To get it undone, he'll need some time. Right now, he's too focused on celebrating."

"Maybe." Oscar nodded. "But if that was me, I'd just rip the bag and grab the diamond."

"Trust me, fish. Pierre can't stand that Grandma gave me that premium thief's bag and he got that *one-of-a-kind* sweater. His dream is to steal it and flaunt it at every family reunion." She looked determined. "That will not happen."

They watched from the dock as Pierre continued to dance. The sound of the waves slapping the boats made Ophelia yawn. She longed to be at home in her own bed, getting the beauty sleep she deserved.

"Hey, Ophelia? Do you like the scuba suit I made?" Oscar asked out of the blue. Ophelia stretched.

"It does make me feel rather powerful." She admired herself in the sea's reflection, impressed with Oscar's design. "It's comfortable, too."

"I was thinking that once we're home, I could design a classic cat burglar outfit for you out of really durable fabric. I could make you a custom mask, too—if you want."

She nodded and felt a fizzle of something un-familiar. Comradery?

"I'd like that. Where did you learn about fashion?" she asked.

Ophelia could see Oscar's grin through his S.P.I.T. "I was always interested in designing things—fashion included! And the feeling when I come up with an outfit and integrate the perfect gadg—"

The lights on the yacht started to go out, one by one. Oscar's (already very bulgy) eyes got wide. "I think Pierre is going to bed!"

Ophelia took a deep breath. "All right, fish. Himalayan Heist part *deux* kicks in *now*. Lead the way through the water. This suit better not leak."

"It won't! I'm the best scientist and inventor you'll *ever* meet."

Ophelia's determination won out over her dread, and she jumped into the water behind Oscar. She was breathing hard to keep up with his swimming fins, but the suit gave her buoyancy and kept her dry.

Once at Pierre's boat, they found the ladder and silently climbed aboard.

"Watch where you step!" Oscar whispered. Mismatched and tarnished lanterns, tacky pictures, and ugly knickknacks lined every available space. "With all this junk, I'm surprised this yacht hasn't sunk."

"We can only hope," Ophelia replied, "that its sinking will happen soon—after we're long gone, of course."

Naturally, Stealth was Ophelia's middle name (really, that's her middle name) and as Oscar stood guard, she tiptoed her way inside around Pierre's trinkets. Room by room, she searched for her bag. Alas, it was nowhere to be found. There was only *one room* left to search. She returned to the fish.

"My bag must be in his bedroom," she reported.

Oscar was optimistic. "Well, it's a good thing you're a cat burglar. Just remember to be ultra-quiet! And fast!"

"It's not that easy," Ophelia admitted. "My whole family is known for sleeping lightly. If I even breathe inside his room, Pierre will wake up. But I might have an idea." Ophelia beckoned for Oscar to come around the side of the boat. "Pierre left his window open. . . ."

Sure enough, through the porthole in his bedroom, they could see a nodded-off Norman and a snoring Pierre hugging Ophelia's bag. "Look what he's snuggling! My Captain Claw-some action figure!" she exclaimed with fury. "I want it back!"

She looked around the deck and grabbed a fishing rod. "Can you use one of these, Oscar? You seem very precise."

Oscar gasped. "Never! It's against my principles."

"Please?" Ophelia asked him.

With disdain, Oscar stared at the fishing rod. "Nope." The fish held his ground. "I'm not doing it. But you go ahead. If you cast it at just the right angle, you'll have no trouble."

Behind them, the engine of the boat started to rumble, and they heard the anchor being pulled up. They were out of time!

"HISS! I have to leave Captain Claw-some here." As she cast a perfect line and hooked her bag, Ophelia whispered, *I'll get you back one day,* Captain Claw-some!"

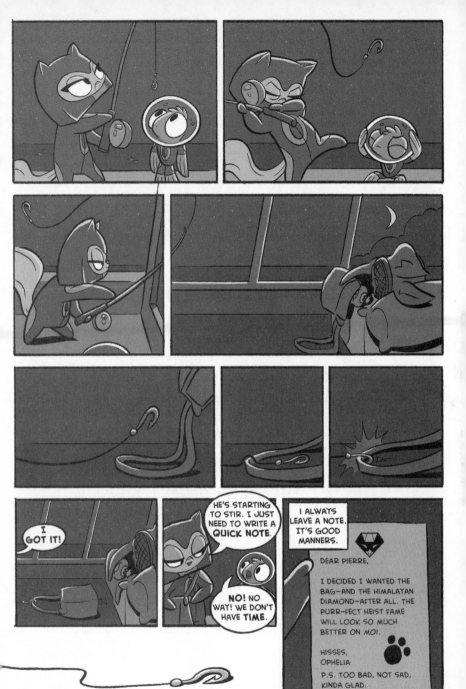

179

Ophelia carefully folded her note into a miniature paper airplane and sent it sailing through Pierre's bedroom window. It hit his forehead and got stuck in his unibrow. He belted out an angry howl as Ophelia and Oscar dove back into the water and headed for shore.

Dry as a bone inside her scuba gear, Ophelia happily swam behind the fish, the gem once again hers. She couldn't be sure, but Ophelia thought they swam right past a boat with the CCIA logo on its stern.

When they were safely on land, the pair made their way to the airstrip at Le Havre and Ophelia arranged for a tiny chartered plane. "Please get us over to Brussels, ASAP!" Ophelia told the pilot. "We have a rather important party to attend."

"Stay classy, world."

—Ophelia von Hairball V

15

CRIMINAL MEWS-TERMIND

Remember this! Dramatic entrances—or exits—always matter," Ophelia said, admiring her fabulous new wingsuit.

"Well, you better hope the wind doesn't work against us. We're racing the clock here. As you requested, I put in a call to MEW to let her know you got the gem. She's expecting you onstage in ten minutes."

"I'm never late. It's a fact. Therefore, the wind shall cooperate fully. Look at the amazing things this breeze is doing to my fur!"

As she flew through the clouds, Ophelia practiced her Purr-fect Heist Competition speech. She was careful not to move her lips, because Oscar had attached a video camera to her helmet so she could take stunning aerial selfies.

"Look down, Ophelia! Everyone's waiting for us!" Oscar exclaimed. "I bet the FFBI committee is surprised we got the diamond! And with only eight minutes to spare!"

The earth got closer and closer, and Ophelia

coached Oscar on his landing pose. "This is important, Oscar. Right when you touch the ground, turn your left side away from the cameras, then smile. Ready, set, SMILE!" They hit the patch of grass together, but Oscar lost his balance and rolled into some nearby shrubs.

Ophelia landed perfectly (she did, after all, have many years of practice), and her grin was as bright as any gem she'd ever nabbed.

Ophelia looked around and wasn't disappointed with the efforts of the FFBI celebration committee. Because it was the fifth-year anniversary of the big competition, the party was fancy to the next level. The grounds were magnificent. She wanted to sprint to the stage and claim her prize but held back and strutted slowly up the aisle so she could take it all in.

"Good morning! Pink punch for you?" A server offered her a diamond-shaped glass.

"Don't mind if I do." She smiled. "What lovely mew-sic." She paused as a troupe of talented mew-sicians played in front of her.

A party host fluttered by. "Did you get your swag bag yet? Don't miss out on the sparkle!"

"I make it my mission to *never* miss any sparkle." Ophelia noted that some of the greatest cat burglars in the world were there (and dressed to the nines). Right before she got to the stage, Ophelia stopped to fix her fur. She took a deep breath. She was ready.

"Excuse me, excuse me!" A short chap with odd facial features and plenty of accessories blocked the red-carpeted stairs.

CONGRATULATIONS! MEW INFORMED ME THAT YOU ARE THE WINNER THIS EVENING. MAY I PLEASE TAKE THE DIAMOND?

Ophelia raised a perfect eyebrow at him. "You want to take the diamond? I already did that!" She winked.

"Hee-hee! Yes. Of course, I don't mean *take* it. The FFBI requires that I *authenticate* it. You know, to make sure it's not fake. After I give the committee the word that it's the real deal, you'll be presented with your well-deserved Purr-fect Heist trophy."

Ophelia opened up her bag and handed him the jewel. "Careful. It's heavy!"

He held it in both hands. "It's lovely! Again, congratulations. I'll be right back!"

I HAVE TO PRACTICE MY **LANDINGS!**

HEY, WHO WAS **THAT?**

THE **FFBI GEMOLOGIST!** HE'S AUTHENTICATING THE DIAMOND TO MAKE SURE IT'S **REAL.**

IT'S TIME FOR THE **STAGE,** OSCAR!

O-O-OPHELIA. LOOK! OH NO! THE **UNIBROW!**

OPHELIA! IT'S **PIERRE!** YOU JUST GAVE THE HIMALAYAN DIAMOND TO PIERRE!

"Keep your focus sharp and your claws sharper."

—Ophelia von Hairball V

16

FIN

With an admirable amount of drama, Oscar flopped onto the ground, and his tail slashed back and forth in frustration. His frantic movements caused his S.P.I.T. to fill with bubbles. "After all that! You just handed the diamond to your conniving cousin! He's going to win!"

"Wow! Nice fin-flips," Ophelia complimented

him. "So theatrical! Have you ever thought of a career on the stage?"

"Aren't you upset?" he barked. "Think about what he's DONE! Pierre stole your mail! He fish-napped me! He made you SWIM! And now the rotten scoundrel is going to take your PRIZE—your FAME!!"

Ophelia crossed her paws and watched as the gemologist (aka Pierre) tripped up the stairs and (accidentally) mopped the floor with his massive eyebrow.

"It's too much! I can't watch!" Oscar piped up. He held his fins over his S.P.I.T.

"Ah, but you must watch," she assured him. "In fact, let's get closer."

Once Pierre made it to the middle of the stage, he handed the gem to the *real* FFBI authenticator. Ophelia walked calmly toward the stage, and the crowd quieted as it sensed an infamous rivalry was about to come to a delightfully tense confrontation. It would be such a scandal if Pierre took the prize this year! Oscar followed Ophelia to the bottom of the stairs, where they stood together to watch.

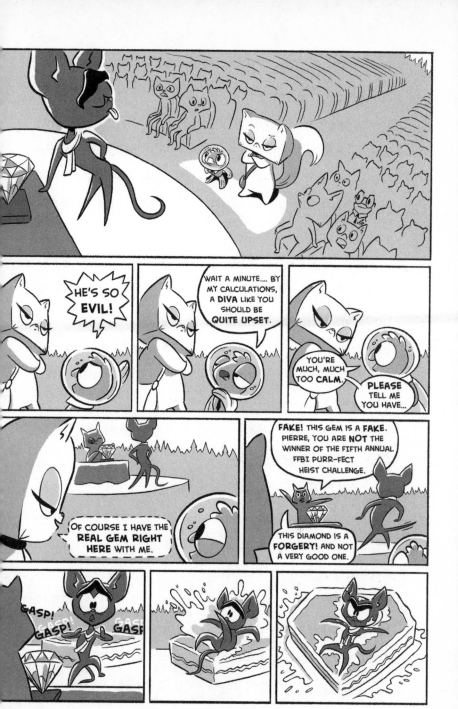

Pierre's eyes caught Ophelia's and he shook with fury. "You!" he hissed. "What did you do?!"

Everyone onstage turned to see who Pierre was talking to. As if surprised by the attention, Ophelia gave a little wave. "Oh, hello," she purred. "I do believe I have the real Himalayan diamond here."

She walked up the stairs and held the magnificent gem above her head for the world to see. (She made sure the light was shining through it to produce beautiful rainbows on her face.) The *real* gemologist took out his loupe and studied the gem. With his nod, there were more flashbulbs and the crowd went wild. It was a divine moment—indeed, almost as divine as the one and only Ophelia von Hairball V.

"Ophelia von Hairball V of Burglaria! We present to you the FFBI's fifth Annual Purr-fect Heist trophy. Speech!"

With an air of confidence and in a regal pose she held for all the cameras to capture, Ophelia stood at the podium with Oscar by her side. "Thank you so much. It's tough to be a cat burglar with class these days. And yet, despite all the obstacles I face"—she looked to Oscar—"the obstacles *we* face . . . we somehow figure things out in fabulous ways. Although I normally work alone, I would like to say thank-you to all my associates and especially my inventor, Oscar Fishgerald Gold."

Beside her, Oscar beamed.

After all the flashbulbs died down, Oscar was blinking furiously. "Remind me to spray my S.P.I.T. with antiglare solution." He looked up at his feline paw-rtner in crime. "Ophelia, thank you for the recognition. One question, though." He lowered his voice to a whisper. "How did you get a second diamond?"

"A great burglar is always prepared, my fine fish. I had a decoy diamond the whole time. Why do you think I was so insistent on taking my bag off the garbage barge?"

"Where will you put your newest gem?" Oscar asked.

OPHELIA VON HAIRBALL V

WINNER OF THE
FIFTH ANNUAL PURR-FECT
HEIST COMPETITION

"Sadly, it's a bit heavy to wear. Perhaps I'll put it in the kitchen for a while—maybe in the fruit bowl—before I return it to the Mew-seum."

"So ..." He looked at her hopefully. "Remember how you said I could have a manicure if you took me on a heist? Stealing the diamond back from Pierre *totally* counts. But since I don't have claws, will you promise to take me on the next adventure instead? What *is* our next adventure?"

"Our next adventure? I personally need a very long nap," Ophelia said.

"I was thinking we could partner up on another heist really soon?"

There was an awkward pause. "Oscar, I value your talents. You're inventive, and your fashion sense is divine. But you do understand that you're *never* coming on a mission with me *ever* again, don't you?"

"What? Why? Coming where? Where are you going next? Because if it's Switzerland, I'm in! I've been practicing my ski moves. I'll make P.U.G. a custom snowboard and we can all go. . . ."

"How many times do I have to tell you, cat? P.U.G. doesn't run on batteries. It's solar-powered. If you want to stop the robo-dog, you'll have to steal the sun."

"Don't tempt me, fish." She winked at him.

All the way back to Ophelia's lair, from the basket of a very fancy hot-air balloon, Oscar pretended he was on a ski hill, his little fins jumping over imaginary moguls. Ophelia managed to ignore him and enjoyed a catnap.

"Sometimes you win and sometimes you lose.
But if you're me, you always win."

—Ophelia von Hairball V

EPILOGUE

FFBI CAT BURGLAR TIP: The world is filled with claw-some surprises. You never know where you might find the purr-fect pair of gloves, a lovely smile, new shoes, or even an unlikely sidekick for an unexpected adventure.

ACKNOWLEDGMENTS

"*Neil! Wake up!*" This series was born in the middle of the night with a ridiculous question about a goldfish. It was the wrong question, but the answer morphed into a bunch of unexpected stuff, like a multitude of Ophelia and Oscar sketches on sticky notes all over the house and countless hours of writing while sitting on the bleachers of many (stinky) middle school basketball courts. This journey has been an unwavering commitment to what-ifs and whimsy, and we couldn't have done it alone.

For Sam, Max, Zach, and Jake—we want you to know that even though we sometimes have our heads in made-up worlds, we love the real-life world with you the best. For our family and friends—we're so happy you let us (and our overactive imaginations) take up space in your lives. And for librarians everywhere—especially Sharon Bede and Sherry Nasedkin—thank you for being the unsung heroes and tour guides to endless worlds.

Thank you to our supersavvy agent, the one-and-only Gemma Cooper of the Bent Agency. We're so lucky to have your brains, instinct, and love of goldfish backing us. To Erin Stein—our brilliant, fabulous, claw-some editor/publisher at Macmillan's bold Imprint—your insight and feedback make this series (and us!) so much better. Gemma and Erin, the gratitude we have for you both (and your incredible teams) is grand and everlasting.

ABOUT THE AUTHOR & ILLUSTRATOR

DEANNA KENT and **NEIL HOOSON** have worked on books, brand and marketing campaigns, and interactive experiences. Deanna loves twinkle-lights, black licorice, and Edna Mode, and she may be the only person on the planet who says "teamwork makes the dream work" without a hint of sarcasm. Neil is king of a Les Paul guitar, makes killer enchiladas, and really wants aliens to land in his backyard. By far, their greatest creative challenge is raising four (very busy, very amazing) boys. Snazzy Cat Capers is their first chapter book series.

snazzycatcapers.com

LOOK FOR THE NEXT MISSION!

Ophelia von Hairball V
of Burglaria

— *in* —

KEEP READING FOR AN EXCERPT!

1

NEED FUR SPEED

It was hot enough to fry catnip on the sidewalk, but nobody paid attention to the snazzy feline sauntering down the Las Vegas strip in her massive motorcycle helmet and protective leather outfit.

"Hey, fancy pants! Watch it!"

Daydreaming, the disguised Ophelia wasn't

paying attention to where her fur-tastic tail was flicking, to and fro.

"WHOAA!" One particularly sassy tail flick knocked over a cart packed to the brim with glitter-bombs. As the sparkly packages smashed onto the road, a multicolored explosion made the street shine and shimmer.

"Oops!" Ophelia stopped to fix the disaster her overenthusiastic tail had caused. "So sorry." She helped the owner stand the cart back up. Surveying the sparkle, she handed over some money to pay for the merchandise. Ophelia smiled. "May I just say . . . this street looks much more fabulous—as does everything—covered in glitter!"

With the kind of flair she normally saved for masquerade balls and wingsuit landings, the infamous Ophelia and her floofy tail continued past a giant pirate ship, a gurgling fountain, massive lion statues (which elicited an involuntary meow from Ophelia), and even a replica of the Empire State Building. Finally, she arrived at her hotel: a great big pyramid. It was a grand spectacle! *Just like me.* She smiled to herself, then checked her watch and felt a whisker-twitching thrill. It was almost time! In just moments, she'd have—

Buzz. Garble. "Ophebrrrzxxxx. OPHELRIXRASCOBZ!"

As Ophelia entered the hotel lobby, a series of high-pitched screeches through the motorcycle helmet receiver made her jump. She couldn't take the helmet off—it was a purr-fect disguise! Ophelia felt around for an off switch but instead found only a mysterious gold button on the outside strap. Ophelia knew better than to push it.

"OPHELIA!" The shrill, aquatic voice on the other end grew a little bit clearer. But it didn't sound particularly happy, so Ophelia tried to ignore it. Right now she had zero time for a fish inventor who was (more than likely) mad at her.

Her silent treatment didn't stop the fish from nattering in her ear. "Ophelia von Hairball V! Hello? Are you there? Helloooo? Wow. Um. Are you ignoring me?" Oscar asked. Ophelia imagined his little fins flapping with frantic frustration. "Seriously, Ophelia, if you can hear me, I've been trying to find you for *days*. Your signal showed up in Chicago, Istanbul, Kelowna, and Tokyo. Did you—?"

"Yes." Ophelia interrupted him. "Yes, yes, *yes*," she confessed. (Sometimes it's easier to just confess.) "There was a row of identical motorcycle helmets on the highest shelf in your lab. I nabbed them, turned on their beacons, boxed up each one, and mailed them to different cities around the globe."

Oscar sounded stunned. "Why in the name of Poseidon would you do *that*?"

"To be really honest, it was a rather desperate attempt to have some alone time. But you found me. I was fairly confident I'd turned off the beacon in *this one*, though."

"Hrumph. Yes, but I include backups in most of my designs," Oscar told her.

A note of admiration crept into Ophelia's voice. "You're rather sneaky, aren't you?"

Oscar Fishgerald Gold was Ophelia's seventeenth inventor. She'd worked very hard to ditch all of her previous sidekicks, as she preferred to burgle on her own. Before Oscar showed up on the doorstep of her lair, she had rejected sixteen inventors for a variety of *very* valid reasons.

HUGH   CHARLIE

#2. REJECTED FOR NEVER BLINKING AND MAKING LOUD CAR NOISES

#7. SENT BACK FOR CONSTANTLY TERRORIZING THE VEGETABLE GARDEN (AND THOSE MESSY PELLETS!)

ADDISON   NORMAN

#10. FOR CHEATING AT MEW-NOPOLY AND DISLIKE OF BLACK LICORICE

#16. FOR HIS TERRIBLE SINGING, OUT-OF-CONTROL BUG PHOBIA, AND THOSE ENDLESS KNOCK-KNOCK JOKES

Known for her legendary capers, Ophelia von Hairball V was the Furry Feline Burglary Institute's number-one cat burglar. *Other* burglars seemed to need (and even want) inventors, but Ophelia took special pride in upholding the classy, time-honored traditions of the FFBI *alone*. Until Oscar, she'd managed to stay 100 percent inventor-less. She'd tried to return him when he'd first arrived, too. But MEW, director of the FFBI, had insisted that she keep him. To be fair, Oscar had proven himself quite useful with his superior gear, gadgets, and fashion designs. But Ophelia still liked to work solo.

Most FFBI cat burglars (especially the elite ones) treated each heist as an opportunity to hone their skills. They performed purr-fect crimes with a touch of elegance and a dash of dare. It was all about the thrill of the chase. And (though it sometimes took a bit longer to return very, very pretty things), they gave back what they pilfered.

The exception? The FFBI's *second-best* burglar, Pierre von Rascal of Thievesylvania, who was (regrettably) Ophelia's nefarious cousin and

archenemy. He was not classy in *any* way. Ever since they'd been kittens, he'd been jealous of Ophelia.

Oscar's voice crackled loudly. "You *can't* ignore me, Ophelia! I've disabled the mute button on all your built-in receivers."

Ophelia rolled her (lovely) eyes. "Please get out of my ear, fish-face. I'm on vacation—I *deserve* a holiday! Some shopping, some pampering"—she looked down at her claws—"and a manicure! I'm spoiling myself." She didn't mention that she'd been mixing a *teensy* bit of business with her fun.

"A vacation? What kind of FFBI cat burglar leaves for vacation without telling their paw-rtner in crime, their soulmate in crime capers?!"

"'Soulmate in crime capers'? Stop it. You're my inventor, Oscar," she reminded him.

"One minute I'm krilling myself to craft you a swanky disguise, and the next minute I'm alone. Are you *really* not going to steal a single thing in Las Vegas? You're just enjoying a heist-free holiday?"

"Well," Ophelia conceded, looking at all the

glitz and glamour surrounding her, "there are a *few* sparkly baubles here and there. I *could* be persuaded to come home with a souvenir."

"Sounds like I should be wherever you are," Oscar pouted.

"You know that glorious Mini-Ultra-Teeny-Tiny Sticker Cam you constructed last week?"

"The M.U.T.T.S.C.?! Sure. It has real potential! But it hasn't been tested yet."

"Well . . . I saw it in your lab, and it looked quite functional," Ophelia told him. "In fact, it looked so *fin*-tastic that I brought it with me. It's attached to the divine motorcycle helmet I'm wearing. You can test it now, if you'd like. Go on," Ophelia prodded him. "Start it up so you can see everything I see in real time. That's almost as good as being here!"

"Well, it's *something*," Oscar retorted. "But it's NOT almost as good as being there. And just so you know, I will be triple-locking my lab from now on. I think it's only fair that if you want to use my inventions, you must take me with you—I want in on the action!"

"Oh, Oscar," Ophelia sighed. "A triple-locked door? You're kitten me. Too easy. Anyhow, you'd hate the desert. Personally, I think the lack of water here is *divine*. But you'd be a puckered-up, dried-out prune fish in no time." She chuckled at the thought.

"You know better than anyone how well my S.P.I.T. works!" Oscar's Small Portable Inter-water Tank invention allowed him to be on dry land for long periods of time. "And last time, in Paris, you promised you'd take me on the next heist!"

She shook her head. "No. You *wanted* me to promise. But I did nothing of the sort."

"Stop with the tantrum and turn on the helmet camera so you can see my genius at play," Ophelia suggested.

"Okay," Oscar sighed and connected the camera's signal to his lab's big screen. The fish could see everything through Ophelia's helmet camera. "Nice! The M.U.T.T.S.C. works well! You're live."

Ophelia swiveled her head so Oscar could get a panoramic view. She imagined Oscar back at home, his little fish-face squashed to the monitor, hoping to see every detail.

"Good picture. Ultra HD, 4K video quality. Um, Ophelia? Why are there a zillion balloons directly above your head? You detest balloons!"

While it was true that balloons usually made her fur stand on end, for this heist to work, Ophelia was depending on them.

"Wait a second. Are you in a pyramid?!" Oscar questioned.

"Why, yes. A purr-amid of sorts," she revealed. She heard the fish typing. He was an excellent researcher.

"Have you pinpointed my location yet?" she asked.

"Of course." The key-clicking got faster. "Nevada. The Luxor Hotel on the Las Vegas Strip?"

Ophelia grinned.

"I'm scanning the hotel's guest list now," he told her. "I bet I can guess what you're trying to steal! Horace B. Fuzzbuttsworth is checked in with his prized Rolex collection. . . . Or, wait! Queen Basta is there, too—with the incredible pearls she won at the Sotheby's auction last week. . . ."

"But you know I prefer old-fashioned timepieces. And I already have exquisite pearls. They're in my secret lair. Hmm. I should wear those pearls again soon. Would you mind dusting them while I'm out of town?"

"Dust? I think not! I'm a *senior* inventor! I have more IQ points than you have hats!" He sighed.

Ophelia moved her head around to give Oscar one more good look at the hotel lobby. "Anyway, I'm not here for the pearls. You're missing the

obvious, fish! Remember the challenges the FFBI issued after the last heist?"

"I've got them here," Oscar told her, confused.

"This mini Vegas vacay was a purr-fect excuse to check off another priceless treasure. I do need to stay ahead of the other burglars. Especially Pierre. That scoundrel—"

"GASP!" The gilled gadget guru sucked in his breath as he suddenly figured out the real reason Ophelia von Hairball V of Burglaria, cat burglar extraordinaire, was at the Luxor Hotel in Las Vegas, Nevada.

Join Ophelia for all her snazzy adventures!

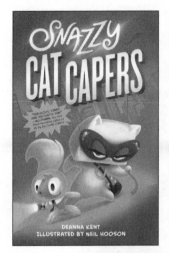

MYSTERIOUS CAPERS BAFFLE SCOTLAND YARD

TWO MORE CROWN JEWELS DISAPPEAR AS BURGLAR LEAVES POLITE THANK-YOU NOTE

POLICE SAID THEY HAVE NO CLUES ABOUT THE MOST RECENT HEIST, EXCEPT FOR A POLITE NOTE LEFT BEHIND IN THE SAFE.

QUESTIONS ABOUT RARE PAINTING

NEW RUMORS EMERGE ABOUT LEGENDARY CATS PLAYING CARDS

MEW-SEUM CURATORS FROM AROUND THE GLOBE MET THIS WEEK IN A SECRET LOCATION TO GO OVER MOUNTING EVIDENCE THAT THE INFAMOUS CATS PLAYING CARDS PAINTING IS MORE THAN A MYTH.

ONE EXPERT, WHO WANTED TO REMAIN ANONY-MEWS, SAID SHE'S HEARD THE PRICELESS PAINTING IS "WITHOUT A DOUBT, RIGHT UNDER OUR WHISKERS." ONLY TIME WILL TELL IF THE PAINTING SHOWS UP IN THE PAWS OF A COLLECTOR.

STOLEN BLACK DIAMOND RETURNED!

PRIVATE COLLECTOR STUNNED TO HAVE GEM RETURNED VIA REGULAR MAIL

"I'M JUST THRILLED IT'S HOME!" SAID THE OWNER OF THE RARE BLACK DIAMOND. "IT WAS SENT BACK ON AN EXQUISITE PILLOW!"

PRICELESS FIRST EDITION TAKEN

VIDEO CAPTURES GRACEFUL, SHADOWY THIEF STUDYING MAPS OF MYTHIC CITIES BEFORE LEAVING CRIME SCENE.